War Is Not Suitable For Children

Judith O'Connor

War Is Not Suitable For Children

and other stories

Acknowledgements

These stories, apart from the few based on my own family, are purely fictiorial and do not relate to real people. They have come to me from my experiences over many years throughout my life. For that, I thank the people and circumstances that have triggered my imagination.

I would like to thank the Society of Women Writers, the Women Writers group and Writing NSW for giving me feedback and encouragement over a number of years. Also to Erica Gray, Judy Pettingell and Pamela Irving who kindly gave up their time to read a selection of the stories. And to Sandy Bresic for her creative talents.

My own children and grandchildren, probably unknowingly, have kept me on track for persevering with writing these stories when I strayed from the task.

I also thank Stephen Matthews OAM of Ginninderra Press for his encouragement and support along the way.

War Is Not Suitable For Children and other stories
ISBN 978 1 76109 645 7
Copyright © text Judith O'Connor 2024
Cover image: Nati from Pexels

First published 2024 by
GINNINDERRA PRESS
PO Box 3461 Port Adelaide 5015
www.ginninderrapress.com.au

Contents

War is Not Suitable for Children

Stefan and I are driving up a shallow riverbed in the backblocks of the wilderness of New Zealand. Sharp rocks, pebbles and stained driftwood everywhere. Fetid smell of rotting timber and dank mud. The river is narrow and the kauri forest entwined with climbing vines reaches down on either side. I feel extremely uneasy. It's eerily quiet except for the crackling sound of the uneven crunches of the tyres as they slip and slide over the gravel and stones of the slippery water course. Fortunately, the river is not running high, reaching mid-tyre in some places and a trickle in others. I'd agreed to the trip in the hope it might work a miracle and make me want to stay married.

The going is slow and it's clear we are in a tricky situation, especially as the car is, ridiculously, a low-slung sports Mercedes, built for the autobahns and cafés of Germany, not this riverbed in the backblocks of the South Island. It's one of Stefan's few indulgences, buying himself a car he loves, from the country of his birth, Germany. He was seven years old when war broke out in 1939, living in what was later called Yugoslavia, a country with a range of ethnic groups hostile to the Germans. His father joined the German army.

'It was compulsory, and we lost touch. They told us he'd been shot but he turned up after the war when I was about sixteen years old. He was a stranger.' Any emotion had been wrung out of Stefan long ago. He could have been talking about a train timetable.

At first, things weren't too bad (I've checked the histories) but when the tide turned and the Russians took over, he and his mother, sister and grandmother were rounded up and shoved into an internment camp.

'We were Germans in an allied country, the Russians were fighting with the British.'

As a young woman, I was ignorant of the impact the war had on his life. I'd grown up in a sheltered backwater in suburban Sydney. I knew that two of my uncles had been in the army and I had a vague idea they'd been in New Guinea. But we'd been on the winning side and it seemed to me that was all I needed to know.

Things were bad (again, I've read the stories; he doesn't talk about it). Deaths, hunger and finally escape by walking at night overland to Germany, sleeping during the day and travelling by night. Stefan's grandmother didn't make it; she died of typhoid in one of the camps and Stefan, who was barely eight years old, had to haul her body to the front of the barracks when the death cart came round. It was the start of his hatred of the British and the prejudices and defences he was to carry all his life. He forever hated gypsies, communists, Serbs and Hungarians. Not to mention the Jews.

Schooling had been out of the question for all but a few lame years. 'Most of the teachers were fighting the war. I was fourteen years old before I could write my name,' he told me in a rare moment of closeness.

His expression had been impossible to fathom. I didn't know what to say so I said nothing, although the shock and sadness has stayed with me to this day. He put his determination to never have to hang his head again and the raw skills that got him through the war to good use. By the time we met in New Zealand decades later, he had built up a prosperous electrical business and, along with property investments, was a wealthy man. The irony was bitter sweet. Now he signs cheques for many thousands of dollars, I thought.

*

As we rattled and bumped our way up the waterway that Stefan would not allow to beat him, my mind flew back to our first encounter many years before. I was working for a major bank in Wellington with an American woman, Veronica. We were secretaries. To my eyes, she was a sophisticated redhead with a twangy accent and fashionable habits and tastes. I loved the way she opened her burnished silver cigarette case, pulled out a Rothman's, flashed her faux-jewelled lighter, and tilted her head ever so slightly to puff out just the right amount of smoke. We were in our early twenties, she on a working holiday. And me, a sheltered Australian who couldn't afford the fare to England, but who had scraped enough together to cross the Tasman.

It was through my friendship with Veronica that I met Stefan. One evening, as we were covering our typewriters and gathering our things, she suggested we go to the local YMCA weekly indoor badminton game in a church hall at the end of Molesworth Street. You have to remember this was the 1960s and in a backwater like Wellington the pickings for socialising were slim.

My first sight of him was under harsh neon lights, a slim, good look-ing man, dashing around with as much energy and bounce as the white-feathered shuttlecock. The room was sparsely furnished. Peeling paint, two cracked windows. A table with a check tablecloth holding a steaming tea urn, cups, saucers and plate of mixed biscuits. Looking down with a steely eye was a photo of Queen Elizabeth II sitting side-saddle on a black horse. Stefan was thirty-two years old and I was twenty-two. I don't think he even noticed me that night. His eyes were all for Veronica.

*

The next day at our typewriters with nothing much to do and after Veronica had touched up her nails and lipstick, we started talking about the coming Easter holiday and the trip she'd suggested we take. There was still snow on the Rimutaka mountains surrounding Wellington and the office was chilly, despite the single-bar radiator at our feet. She was wearing a stylish mohair cardigan with large round buttons with tiny pearls in the centre to match her earrings. The idea was to catch the Greyhound bus to the holiday town of Taupo in the centre of the north island with its expansive freshwater lake, boating activities and strolls around the town. We'd stay in a cheap cabin, and hopefully find some fun and social activity.

'Guess what?' She swivelled her chair to face me.

I looked up, feeling in good spirits at the thought of our few days away.

'Stefan is going the same way as us at Easter. He's driving to a holiday hut he's got nearby and he said he'd give us a lift. So we won't have to bother with the Greyhound.' She turned back to her desk, picking up a folder marked 'outgoing correspondence'.

She'd flicked me off as casually as the ash on her cigarette and her focus had shifted without a thought from a few days' away with me, to (hopefully) a romantic adventure with this new man, Stefan. I was furious and disappointed, dreading the days ahead. A threesome was not what we'd agreed.

When Stefan picked us up, she made sure she got into the front seat, leaving me to struggle with the luggage in the back. The wind rushing past the windows stopped me hearing their conversation. After a while, I gave up and concentrated on the rapidly changing scenery. From high-rise buildings to farmland and peaked mountains. Sheep and grass. The black clouds that had been stealing across the sky about an hour after we'd left Wellington burst and great fistfuls of rain pounded the windscreen.

Stefan, intent on watching the blurry shapes and shadows through the windscreen, shot a quick glance at Veronica. 'I've got an idea. Let's get out of this. There's a hunter's forestry hut not far from here. We can stay the night and still be in Taupo early tomorrow.'

Without waiting for an answer, he made a sharp swing to the left and before Veronica had time to think (I was not consulted), we were slipping and sliding along a narrow dirt track.

After about an hour, the rain eased and we came to a muddy stop at the front of a crude wooden hut not far from snow-capped Mount Ruapehu. Stefan jumped out and strode towards the hut and, with a hefty push with his shoulder, opened the door. The hut was as you'd expect for emergency accommodation for forestry workers. Cramped and dirty, cobwebs, mice droppings. Double bunks. Mouldy mattresses. Stumps of candles and a bucket to collect water from the river.

Stefan got a fire going and produced some dehydrated food from his rucksack. I'd never tasted dried meat but, with long and deliberate chewing, managed to swallow enough to keep the hunger away. Veronica was aghast at our surroundings and after one look at the stringy food, grabbed her cigarettes and said she wasn't hungry. I'd never seen her say no to food before. It wasn't long before her eyes itched and she had the sneezes. Her mood turned black. Nonetheless, she grabbed the bottom bunk, opposite Stefan. They were within arm's reach. I was left with the top bunk above Stefan. I could sense the sexual energy in the air. I was uneasy and wished I hadn't come.

Before we went to sleep, Stefan said something like 'I'll be up early, when the sun comes up. Hunting for rabbits. So don't worry if you don't see me.'

He leaned his rifle next to the door. I'd never seen one before and worried that it might be loaded. Within minutes, his breath deepened and he'd fallen asleep.

I hadn't noticed the small mud-stained window at the top of my bunk or the tattered cotton rag pulled across as a curtain. Or that the window was open at the bottom. Sometime during the night, I started tossing and turning. My back felt like a block of ice had been slipped inside my T-shirt. I realised later that it was the piercing cold from the snows of Mount Ruapehu coming through the opened window straight down my sleeping bag. My thrashing around had obviously woken Stefan in the bunk below. Before I knew what was happening, he'd stood up. In the half light, I saw his shadowed face. He put his hands under me and lifted me down into his bunk, then got in next to me. I had never lain in bed with a man before. Nothing happened, no sex, no gropings, nothing. Just a nice warm nest-like feeling. The cold disappeared.

Dawn broke, Stefan got up, grabbed the waiting rifle, and was gone looking for hapless rabbits. Veronica woke a few hours later to find me in the bunk opposite where Stefan had been sleeping. She was confused and so was I. Neither of us quite knew how the rearrangement had happened but we both knew things had changed.

By Christmas, Stefan and I were married.

*

My thoughts jar back to the riverbed as a boulder thumps the floor of the car. Stefan's mouth tightens and my anxiety rises. How the hell did I get here? What was I thinking marrying this man of extreme tastes?

OK, I tell myself, I have to accept that Stefan is an adventurer. Deer stalking is his hobby and the roughness and danger of the bush his element. He was adamant that I get involved in all his activities and I, pliable by nature and upbringing, did what I was told. I pushed my tender feet into leather boots, donned layers of warm and wet weather gear and learnt how to bush-bash my way through kauri forests with their tangles of ferns and cabbage trees, even crawling on hands and knees at times. One Christmas, when I was visiting my family in Sydney, he'd written to me.

> I had my best hunting luck ever. I got up at the crack of dawn and about half an hour from the hut I saw a deer looking straight at me. I stood still for what seemed ages. It carried on feeding so I snuck around a bush and calmly aimed at it. As I was ready to pull the trigger, a second one walked right in front of the first one. I felt like yelling get out of the way. But I aimed at the second one and dropped it with the first bullet. Next second, another three deer jumped out from behind bushes. One came straight at me so I shot him first then with the speed of lightning loaded and shot at the third one running down the hill. This one dropped too. Only by moving with the speed of light was I able to reload and shoot the fourth deer. And all this without moving from the spot. It was just like a dream. Although I saw all four lying there I couldn't believe it. Until I went there and cut their throats.

It was not uncommon for Stefan and his mates to spend weeks in areas so remote they had to be dropped in by helicopter, along with food supplies. He had wanted me to go once, to the southernmost part of the country but I backed out after his mates, thank God, told me privately some of the hazards, like the river that had to be crossed by hanging onto a rope and swinging Tarzan-style across to the other side. I still have nightmares.

There were times, however, when I did accompany him as a new bride with nothing more in my heart than the wish to please him. One redeeming thing I always thought (though wisely I kept it to myself) was that deer are in their element in the wilderness and no matter how much we crept and stayed silent, they always knew we were near. So I wasn't overly worried when I found myself at the foot of the Kaikoura mountains.

'There's a grassy flat about three kilometres away. We'll go there in the afternoon and climb a tree. Catch them feeding. They won't see us.'

I can't remember climbing and perching in the tree but I recall the quietness and delicacy of the bush and dusky colours that enveloped us as twilight descended. My eyes scanned the soft line where the thick vegetation stopped and the grass flat started, the very edge of two worlds, one secret the other public. Like magic, I saw the outline of a deer emerge, take a few steps, lower its head and start grazing. It was as if it had been superimposed on the scene. We'd done the impossible, tricked one so that we saw it, but it didn't see us. I felt Stefan's excitement coursing through him, his rifle at his side. I waited for the moment when he would pull the trigger and get the trophy he felt he deserved. Instead, he handed the rifle to me.

'You shoot it. It can be your first one.'

He positioned the rifle into my shoulder and I held the end with one hand and curled the fingers of my other hand around the trigger. I lined up the barrel, my line of sight running along its smooth surface, through the notch of the sight device on the end and straight into the body of the grazing animal.

The moment had come. All I had to do was squeeze the trigger. I prepared myself to do what this man, this man I longed to please, wanted. But as I steadied my aim, Stefan's power slipped off and I tuned into my own emotions. I marvelled at the beauty, delicacy of the wild animal, lowering and raising its head as it chewed the grass. Every cell in its body seemed to jump at me. Pulsating. Not so much the big things like bones, organs, head. But the life force in the creature. The pulsations seemed to expand balloon-like and all I could think of was its perfect beauty and vulnerability. I had the power to let it live or die. Was I seriously going to kill it? I pushed the rifle to one side, making sure I bumped a branch of the tree. The noise was slight but enough. The deer vanished as mysteriously as it had emerged, gone forever. Its life had not changed. But mine had. I saw Stefan's love of blood sports for what they were. His lust for killing repulsed me.

But deer were not the only trophies Stefan liked. He had other appetites. As the car tyres slipped and crunched along the water course, my mind flew back to the time we'd unexpectedly come upon a young woman on a three-day trek soon after our marriage. I can still see Stefan's face, full of excitement, body curving towards her with the same pleasure he gets from his Mercedes taking a smooth bend. The woman was asking questions about the track ahead and Stefan, in full stride, was telling her stories and jokes about his last trip. Laughing. Throwing his arms around, playfully pointing his finger at the woman.

'You see –' His accent thickened. 'It's like this –'

I could hear the sexual undertone in his voice.

As he got to the end, he prodded his finger against the woman's chest, every gesture emphasing his story. He finished with multiple guffaws, a flushed face and, as sometimes happens, a few harmless sprays of spit.

This nameless woman dropped out of my life. But not the others that were to follow in the years ahead.

*

It had been his idea, of course, to use the river as a way to get deeper into the bush after the roughly hewn dirt road had petered out. He wanted to reach the foothills of the Rimutakas before nightfall but time is running out. I lift my eyes from the rough terrain and glance at Stefan behind the wheel, mouth tightening, eyes blazing. I'm feeling nervous and worried, not so much because of our precarious situation as the moods that I see cross his brow. Things are not going to plan. I open the window and the icy sprinkles from the river bounce up and sting my cheeks.

There's a sudden loud, fatal crunch and thud. The car is stuck. Stefan gets out, his mood formidable. We lug rough stones from the patchy riverbank to build a makeshift jack to prop the back of the car up so he can see what the trouble is. He wriggles underneath, legs and shoulders disappearing. My eyes linger over the strip of midriff skin, smooth and sensual. Then there's a crunch and sickening thud. The rocks have dislodged and the car has dropped a few centimetres from his chest. He can't move. He tries to push the vehicle upwards so he can wriggle out but he can't get a grip. Our eyes lock. What do I read in his stare? Shock? Fear? Or is he projecting his usual steely control?

'You'll have to help me.' His voice is hard. 'Get this car off me. You have to –'

I stand, suspended over him. He's trapped, we're totally isolated, no eyes around. My mind goes wild. This is my moment to avenge the pain and heartbreak this man, with his twin lusts of butchery and fucking, has wrought on me, shredding my heart as blithely as he skins his hapless prey. I now have the upper hand. Time stands still. It's like I'm in a dream. Drifting and floating. My eyes sweep the surrounding bushland. Lush, dense. Nothing stirs. I glance down at him. Face reddening. Suddenly the air explodes with the screech of a flock of kea landing in a nearby tree. And I snap back to reality. What am I thinking?? I lurch forward and grasp below the car's mud-stained bumper bar. And, God knows where the strength comes from, I lift the dead weight of the back of the vehicle away from him while he pushes upwards, and between us he manages to scramble out.

All is well. I saved him, you might think.

But…I did hesitate.

The Day Harry Left

The fingerprinting, of course, is shaking my bravado. I quickly read the police instructions above the ink-pad on how to do it, and how to get it wrong. The airless smell of the police station hits my nostrils and the harshness of the rows of fluorescent lights beat remorsefully down, leaving no wrinkle on my face unlit. The carpet at the front desk is the colour of old blood.

I try to botch the fingerprinting by curving my fingers on the ink-pad instead of pressing down, but the child of a policewoman standing over me won't have a bar of it.

'The sarge will make you do it again.' She's scolding me, this slip of a girl who's young enough to be my daughter. 'Let's have another go.' She leans forward and presses my fingers into the pad with so much pressure I know there's no monkeying around with her. 'I've only been in the force for nine months.' She gives me a little smile.

I notice her stolid build, large hands. She thinks this is a time for a friendly chat? I turn away.

'I'm studying domestic violence.' She smiles and for one second I think she's going to give me a conspiratorial wink as if she and I are sharing a secret, as if that's why I'm in this bloody police station. She later asks me to read her assignment. Ha.

I feel the gritty, dryness of my hands. I try to calm down, not let my swirling emotions get a grip. To distract myself, I reach for the container of liquid soap next to the ink-pad. It's covered in the smudgy prints of nameless hands that have held it before me. I notice the label Morning Glory. It turns out to be the grossest, rawest detergent ever devised. Like washing your hands with wire. Yet, however much I scrub, I can't get rid of the traces of black ink. I think of Lady Macbeth.

I knew, of course, when I saw the flashing blue lights on the police vehicle on the side of the highway that I was over the limit.

'We're pulling everyone up,' the cop had said. Businesslike, important. His face loomed through the side window of the car like those funny mirrors at Luna Park that make your nose and eyes telescope out at you. He thrust a tube-shaped object at me. 'Blow into this and don't try any tricks. You won't get away with it. You get two goes, that's all.'

Cripes, I thought, was he reading my mind? How did he know I was going to try to botch the test? It was all over in less than a minute.

'Get out, we'll drive your car. You're over the limit. You'll be taken to Hornsby police station and charged.'

My stomach lurched. I'm pretty sure he said arrested, but I'm blocking that out.

There was a long wait in the watch house. No privacy. Six men, I'm the only woman. One of the men is sitting around a corner and I can only see his fat, bare thigh. He's talking to the older man next to him. I hear his loud, drunken slur.

'Jeez, mate, give us a break. I'm fucking stuffed – I'll lose me job – The wife will kill me –'

It's gross. I feel awful.

Eventually, I'm taken aside and interviewed by another startlingly young sergeant who balances a card of printed questions on his knee as he ticks boxes and writes short answers. He holds another piece of paper under each question and moves it slowly line by line down the page like a slow reader in primary school. He's concentrating hard.

'I'd like to say something,' I say.

'At the end.' His voice is sharp. 'One thing at a time.'

I can tell I've irritated him.

Eventually, he looks up and stares at me blankly. 'OK, now.'

'My husband, Harry, left me today.' I feel exposed, humiliated. I'm aware I'm the only woman in the place and an older one at that.

'Oh,' is all he says. His eyes roll upwards with lack of interest and boredom. He stands up and steps towards the door, its brown paint darkened with age and grime. He doesn't speak, just inclines his head impatiently to tell me to follow.

I get up, fatigue washing over me. I'm led into a processing room. There's a sign: *Appointments MUST NOT be worn under any circumstances in the cells.* The MUST NOT is in big, black, capital letters.

'Appointments?' I couldn't resist, I had to ask.

'Oh, that's our gun and other stuff,' the sergeant tells me, tapping the leather holster on his belt.

I notice he's not wearing his appointments. I feel panic. If he's not wearing it, does that mean we're headed for the cells? Instead, he steers me towards a large wooden box structure, like a Dr Who phone box, with a camera and small stool inside. It's pokey and grimy. The whiff of foul air from inside its airless walls float towards me. I realise with dread it's for taking mugshots. Then, don't ask me why, he changes his mind and says he won't bother this time.

'It's like a sausage machine tonight,' he complains as he swaggers off like a man with the weight of the justice system on his shoulders.

I hear his monotone in the next room through the cheap panelling of the walls as he goes down his list of questions with the next law-breaker. I couldn't see any other sausages in the place except myself and one other man who, bizarrely, said he knew me from somewhere. Cripes, no you definitely don't, mate.

I feel nervous. I begin perambulating. Reading, looking, observing, thinking, anything to distract myself. I poke my head around the corner towards the lock-up. I ask what questions I can of the red-headed officer sitting on a chair near the photo box waiting for customers. He's flicking over a newspaper, nodding as he skims the headlines.

'You must get sick of the same old parade of heads lining up?' I ask in a desperate attempt to strike up a friendly conversation with some-one.

'Nah. They're all no-hopers. I push 'em in, click the camera, push 'em out.' He throws the newspaper aside, gets up and heads for the cof-fee machine.

Two ladies with bright orange short tunics over their blouses who remind me of the lollipop ladies outside schools wander around. One comes over and asks whether I'd like to talk about anything. I wouldn't have minded, but her look of pained suffering and the handful of religious pamphlets in her hand puts me off. She asks me whether I want a cup of tea or coffee. I say no.

'You're here for an apprehended violence order, dear?' she asks.

'No, drunk driving.'

She gasps, her eyebrows shooting up. She turns and walks away.

Around three a.m., I'm given another test. This time they tell me I'm OK to go home.

'Have you got someone to pick you up?

'No,' I say. Is there no end to my embarrassment and distress?

The shift has changed and an older, more streetwise police officer on his way to get a round of McDonald's hamburgers for the night duty officers says he'll give me a lift to my car. It's the first touch of human kindness I've had. The tears pour out.

When I get home, I switch on the television to shout out the loneliness and emptiness. The movie is *Carry On Up the Khyber.*

I glance at the newspaper, my eyes zeroing in on an article about an Aussie getting fifty years in a Thai jail for smuggling a teaspoon of heroin.

The exhaustion hits me. I throw it down.

'It's been a long day,' I say to the cat. 'I'm going to bed. You can turn off the TV.'

My Father and Bing Crosby

In the middle of a family lunch at Coogee, a beachside suburb of Sydney, my father slipped away. He walked across the road to a curve of sand at the end of the main beach. He stood gazing at the horizon in the way people do in such places. No one had noticed him leave and I thought at the time it was unusual because he was by no means a solitary man.

I got up from the table and joined him. I had no particular reason, and there we stood, just two people staring out across the ocean.

His eyes were focused far away and he was clearly absorbed in his inner thoughts, a million miles away, transported to another place, another time.

Behind, in the restaurant, the conversation and laughter were going on happily and loudly. It was his granddaughter Eleanor's graduation lunch and most of the family was celebrating. Before he'd walked across the road, he'd been sitting on a seat facing the ocean where he could take in the panorama of curving sand and mesmerising waves. The table was so close, you could hear them breaking, tipping up the sand until they ran out of puff, pausing, then trickling back into the sea. The sky was a blaze of blue, the air sweet.

As he stood gazing out to sea, lost in his own world, it seemed to me he was picking up a presence in the still air. His own presence from many years earlier, when he'd arrived in Australia as a nineteen-year-old youth running away from a dubious past in New Zealand.

He'd cleared out, as he called it, from his family home in Wellington when he was twelve years old. He'd lived as a street kid until the police found him and he'd been sent off to a Catholic school for wayward boys. He'd had his knocks and battles but ended up graduating as dux some six years later with a scholarship to Wellington's prestigious Catholic college, St Patricks.

Maybe it was the clamour and neglect that went with a large Irish Catholic family living in a two-bedroom house, the floggings he got from the Marist Brothers at St Patrick's when he turned up in his uncle's old overcoat instead of the school uniform because his parents had no money, or he didn't have a note from home to explain his absences.

'My mother couldn't read or write, so there was never a note.'

Or, maybe, it was the call of his wandering spirit. I remember, as a child some twenty years later, he'd stop whatever he was doing, usually making or repairing something for the house he was building for us, when Bing Crosby came on the radio singing his 1940 hit song 'Don't Fence Me In'. It triggered something I was too young to understand; the emotion that had caught him unexpectedly was foreign to me, but now, as an adult, I would describe it as a sort of rapture.

> Oh, give me land, lots of land under starry skies above
> Don't fence me in
> Let me ride through the wide open country that I love
> Don't fence me in
>
> I want to ride to the ridge where the west commences,
> Gaze at the moon till I lose my senses
> I can't stand hovels and I can't stand fences
> Don't fence me in.

Eventually, the beatings and humiliation tipped him over the edge and he jumped on a cargo ship for Australia. Even on his deathbed at the age of eighty-six years, he relived the feeling of taking over the wheel in the dead of night. He was hospitalised, struggling for breath, but through the tangle of oxygen and other tubes and devices, I swear I caught a glimpse of that same long-ago expression of open spaces from his Bing Crosby days. He was reliving a moment in his youth, as a young adventurer with the world at his feet.

'The captain needed a sleep. He told me to steer straight ahead, not right or left. It was just me and the whole of the Tasman Sea.'

He arrived in Sydney during the Great Depression and, like many others, went on to walk and ride a bicycle around the east coast looking for work. But when you're nineteen years old and alive for adventure, it's not all bad. The swims in rivers, country dances and freedom to go north, south or west were pretty good.

He'd worked as a day labourer in Canberra in 1930, when men competed with each other for a day's pay, travelled on top of the Cooma Mail train, his face full of black soot, terrified he'd have his head chopped off every time the train sped through a tunnel. He'd carried a swag, camped in showgrounds with hundreds of other unemployed men where the regulation was you had to move on the next day, chopped wood for a loaf of bread and had his twenty-first birthday in Cootamundra, where he was cutting thistles at a sheep station nearby.

It wasn't as if he'd been sad, distracted, in the restaurant that day in Coogee. He'd been having a good time, laughing and telling his usual stories. His eyes, not quite as blue as they had been, were concentrated on the moment, his face spread with pleasure, his speech direct and to the point.

We hadn't spoken to any extent as we'd stood facing the ocean then, suddenly, 'This is where I spent my first night in Australia,' he said, pointing to the narrow curve of sandy beach.

It was a very personal moment, one he had never talked about when I was growing up. What went through his head? It was clearly not simply a momentary 180-degree scan of a pretty scene as a passer-by might have presumed. He was eighty-eight years old, living in Queensland, and he was remembering the beginning of his story, realising the poignancy of finding himself again at this spot. Perhaps he knew it was his full circle, that his beginning was now his ending.

In a few short months, he was dead. I like to think his presence will always be there on that sweep of Coogee beach.

Cross Roads, Cross Purposes

The vasectomy. You wanted it, I didn't.

It wasn't till I started going through my old letters and papers recently that I came across the faded admission form for Calvary Hospital, in Wellington, New Zealand. I can't believe I'd forgotten about it.

I'm sitting at my kitchen table in Sydney all these decades later, gazing out the window at the sway of gum trees, my mind whirling back over the decades.

It's a longish form but only three bits are filled in: your name, written by you in big, bold capitals in dark blue fountain pen ink – I can sense the pressure of your hand pressing into the paper and the force of your personality jumps across the years and wallops me in the eye – then there's the doctor's name and the name of the operation: vasectomy.

The critical part is blank – the signature of *consenting party*, which was me, the wife. It's unsigned, empty, untouched. The doctor, the law in fact, said that you couldn't go through with the operation unless you had the consent of your partner. You could see their point.

There is no date but I remember you appearing at my door. What would it be? Thirty years ago? You had the form in your hand, furious that you could be thwarted in getting what you wanted. Your face was like thunder and you meant business. You came into the living room. We stayed standing. This was no social visit. The furniture and surroundings faded away and just the two of us filled the space.

You were in full force rage, furious that you had to ask for permission, that you, who'd lived a life full of risk, daring and inventiveness, survived the tightrope between life and death as a child in Germany in World War II, who'd had to live every day off your wits, who'd seen and done more than your average sleepy Kiwi – including the doctor – could hold this thing over your head. This flimsy bit of paper that, I see now, represented not just a surgical procedure, but a threat to your iron will, your determination, what made you tick.

I felt for you.

Your body language was fearsome. You scared me with the strength of your anger, fury. Your face was hard, the familiar frown lines etched so deeply they seemed black.

You stood in front of me. You were bristling, crackling.

It looked like I was standing up to you. But I wasn't. I didn't know what to do. I was upset and mortified. My insides were like jelly and my mind in shock.

I had known nothing about your intentions, that you'd had a vasectomy in mind. We'd been separated for some months and you were dealing with the searing rip the only way you knew how. Brute force, throwing punches at some bogeyman inside you.

'Why bring children into the world? Why make them suffer for the way things are. It's better not to be alive.'

What sort of talk was this? Where did this come from?

I can still see the bones of your lean body through your dusty, creased work clothes. The brown trousers, the ever-so-slight curve of your bow legs, the leather belt that wrapped around your waist far enough to reach the second loop of your trousers. Blue shirt, polyester in those days, short sleeves, with a small grey square pattern. Your mother had sent it from Germany, along with the regular Y-front underpants and socks.

Perhaps I should have signed the form and not stood in your way. After all, it was your body, your sperm. Women don't want anyone telling them whether or not they should terminate a pregnancy, it's their body. Was this any different?

Instead, I took the high moral ground. I was young and full of spirit back then. It was a big ask and I didn't want the responsibility. The decision on the future of your genes had been unwillingly thrust, literally, into my hands. And I was not prepared to buy into this one.

'No.' I stood my ground. The issue was black and white in my mind, very Catholic, I was told later. 'I won't sign. It shouldn't be me. I don't want to make that decision.'

We stared at each other, our eyes on fire. But I felt on firm ground.

'I'll give you a divorce, then you won't need my consent. You can do what you like then. I won't have to make the decision.'

I don't remember much more. I guess you must have left with your bit of paper unsigned. No, that can't be right. You must have left it with me because here it is. It's ended up amongst my papers.

Eventually we did divorce but you never had the vasectomy.

Friendly Fire

Marg hadn't meant to burn the house down. It had been an accident. Of sorts. She'd swung past her mad cousin Betty's place on a whim a few months before she and Reg headed north.

She and Betty had got up to a few tricks when they were kids. They were known to police, as the newspapers put it, their escapades escalating from shoplifting to stupid ideas that could have seen them locked up. Nicking bras and nighties is our best bet, Betty used to say at the start. No one's going to strip search a couple of schoolkids. And they were bloody good at it, Marg remembered with a whiff of nostalgia. That was until Betty talked her into the big one. Their last transgression. Stealing a horse from Centennial Park and somehow trying to walk it through the national park to Wollongong to sell for the Kembla Range Golden Cup races. What a hair-brained, disorganised mess that had turned into. Marg blocked out the part about her close brush with the police. Fortunately, they'd ditched the whole idea (and the horse) around Kurnell, caught the train to Katoomba and stayed in a miserable youth hostel for a week until Betty thought it was safe to go home. Jesus! A horse. They were nineteen years old and could have gone to jail for that.

Marg was curious. Her mother had told her stories. 'Betty's gone quite dotty, reckons every time the bloke in the apartment upstairs flushes his toilet, it drops into her bathroom. And she says her phone is tapped and someone pinches her mail.'

They'd been having a family dinner and Marg had felt uncomfortable at the sniggers and jokes flying around the table about her old friend.

'Oh, and she's always seeing Harry lurking around the place,' her mother added. Harry was Betty's long dead brother (also a bit dotty, it must be said). 'She sees him walking in the street, crossing the road, says I lied about his death, even though I took her to the funeral parlour to say goodbye.' Her mother had paused to top up her glass of Pinot Noir.

'There he was.' She glanced at Marg. 'Undeniably Harry. They'd dressed him in a white shirt and beige cardigan buttoned halfway up his chest. His hair was combed and his head was resting on a satin pillow. Betty spent some time with him. The worst thing is,' her mother had lowered her voice, 'she won't go to bed. Ever since Harry died, she's been convinced she has to sleep sitting up and has more or less moved her life permanently onto her old armchair in the lounge room.'

Marg had felt a pang of sympathy for her old friend. Maybe she should drop by and see for herself.

Marg stubbed out her cigarette as she pulled up outside Betty's house and checked she had her mobile phone. Reg would be wondering where she was. The concrete walls were stained with rust streaks from the windows and the entrance darkened by a garage built by the man living in the apartment above. She leant forward and knocked on the door. When there was no response, she had no qualms about giving it a push. It didn't budge but after a shove with her shoulder, it opened enough for her to squeeze through. OK, illegal entry, she thought with a smirk. Just like the old days.

The blast of foul air took her breath away, a mixture of mould, cigarette smoke and Betty's limp underwear drying on a rack in the hallway. She dropped her sunglasses into her handbag and tried to think. She was about to turn back and ring Reg. Get out of this cave-house fast. But just as she swung around towards the door, her eyes adjusted to the gloom and she saw the figure ahead.

Betty. Mounds and rounds of rolling flesh, in her rotting tapestry armchair in front of the blaring television where a clean-cut man was spinning his *Wheel of Fortune*. Patches of yellow and brown stains on the walls from decades of cigarette smoke and lack of ventilation. The windows were taped and Marg remembered her mother had said Betty was scared poison gas would get in.

She noticed a bookcase, with a distinct lean, stacked with mildewed *Reader's Digests*, paperbacks and various knick-knacks including a porcelain Dutch clog with blotchy pink and cream glaze and a photograph of a stodgy man and woman. Betty and her brother Harry? She remembered Betty telling her Harry lived in the country. Gilgandra, she seemed to remember. He would come down on the overnight train to visit Betty. They'd meet under the clock at Central railway station and catch a tram to Randwick races or the Easter Show.

Beyond the gloom, Marg could see into the cluttered, junk shop kitchen, full of dented saucepans and mismatched crockery, green mottled bench top. The mouldy sink with the old gas hot water heater perched on the wall above. The outside casing had once been white, she supposed, but was now a sickly cream, like pale egg yolk. The pilot light flickered away.

She began to panic, realising she'd made a mistake entering Betty's world. They weren't kids any more, getting into a bit of mischief. She thought back over the wild, criminal things Betty had pushed her into all the years they'd been growing up. Marg had resented it even as a kid. But now, as she saw the ugly mess Betty had become, she was full of anger and fury. Betty had been the worst thing that had happened to Marg. Even now, years later, Marg sometimes went off the rails thanks to the criminal imprint Betty had left on her. There'd been a few run-ins with the cops over this and that but she'd manage to talk her way out of being charged. Thankfully, she'd been able to keep it from Reg. The last thing she wanted was for her old life with Betty to cause any trouble now just as she and Reg were about to head north to start their life together.

She badly needed a cigarette. She fumbled around in her handbag until she found a packet of Rothmans and her lighter. The movement caught Betty's eye and Marg knew she'd left it too late to creep out. Betty knew someone was watching.

Marg took a few deep drags and against her better judgement stepped forward towards the figure in the armchair. 'Betty, Betty – it's me, your cousin, Marg.'

Betty turned slowly, struggling to focus. Her unlit roll-your-own smoke in her hand, 'Marg? Is it really you? Me old schoolmate?' She broke into a wheezy laugh. 'Come for a bit of mischief, have you? Like the old days? Yeah, I can see you're still a skinny bitch, still get through a window or two.' Betty's face twisted as her laugh escalated into a racking cough. 'Coppers still after you after our little run-in at Kurnell? You remember, Marg, when you got the wind up after we'd ditched the horse. Where'd you get it from? The rifle. I knew your old man had one but didn't think you'd be smart, or stupid, enough to bring it along.'

Betty raised her head and half-laughed, half-spat into Marg's face, her long hair straggling down her cheeks. 'I can still see your shit-scared face when the coppers got close. What were you thinking, you stupid bitch, firing at them like that? Even if it was above their heads.'

Betty pulled out a torn handkerchief and wiped her nose. It took her a few minutes to get her breath back. 'Running away, stealing a horse was one thing. But shooting at cops? Put us in another class.'

'Cut your stupid talk, Betty. That's ancient history. I never hit anyone and we never got caught, did we? We said it would be our secret. You promised. You promised –' Marg felt prickles on her neck. Stupid, foul Betty. Why was she gabbing on about that wretched time? They'd promised to say it never happened.

'I never snitched on you, Marg. But you put a curse on me. If it hadn't been for you, Harry would come back…' She turned slowly towards the photograph on the bookshelf. 'Harry, come here,' she beckoned with one finger. 'Over here. Talk to me.' Her voice dropped to a whisper.

Marg shifted uneasily on one foot. Who knew what mad pictures and voices were circling in Betty's head?

'Maybe I should dob you in, Marg. Tell the cops what I know and things will come right for me again.' Betty's face twisted into an ugly sneer. 'I hear you've got a boyfriend these days. Trying to make a new start. What would he think if he knew you're a wanted person?'

Betty's mood had turned sour. If there'd been a skerrick of goodwill or old-mateship when she first saw Marg, it had disappeared and instead Marg knew she was looking at a mean-minded, dirty old woman who in her deranged mind was blaming Marg for her own worthless life. Marg felt the anger and loathing swell up inside her. How did she know Betty wouldn't spill the beans and her life with Reg, the only good relationship she'd ever had would vanish in a puff? And, worse, Marg reminded herself, she might well end up in jail.

Betty smiled slowly and held out her nicotine-stained fingers. 'I see you've got your lighter, Marg. Give us a light.'

Get this over, and get out, Marg told herself. She flicked open her lighter, the one she'd picked up from the posh hotel in Kempsey where she and Reg had stayed last Christmas. But as she stepped forward, her foot caught in a rip in the filthy carpet and she shot forward with a frightened cry. The naked flame landed on Betty's lap. Betty yelled and dropped her head to snatch it away. Marg saw Betty's hair dangling over her eyes dangerously close to the flame and knew in that split second what was going to happen. There was one split second when Marg could have sprung forward and made a grab for the lighter. But she didn't. Flames singed the ends of Betty's tangled hair and, within seconds, her whole head was a horrifying halo of flames. A foul smell filled the air as Betty's body fluids spilled onto the cushion beneath her and Marg knew Betty was dead.

The blazing furnace that was virtually cremating Betty's body devoured her tapestry chair within minutes, shot across to the floor-length curtains and through the open door to the kitchen. As Marg ran to her car, she heard the ear-splitting explosion from the gas hot water heater in the decrepit kitchen. She glanced back as the flames shot up the walls of the house, to the roof and into the swirling sky.

She ran for all she was worth, stricken by what had happened. Her mind raced over the whole episode, the memories and experiences they had triggered. Finally settling on Betty's threat to tell Reg about her past.

She flung open the car door and by the time she was buckling her seat belt, a slow smile was spreading across her face.

Her secret was safe.

Betty's death made the six o'clock TV news.

A sixty-seven-year-old woman burned to death in her house today. Police believe the deceased, described by neighbours as reclusive, accidentally started the fire while lighting a cigarette. Police say the state of disrepair of the house contributed to the blaze taking hold. There were no witnesses and no suspicious circumstances.

The Delights of Winter From a Cat's Perspective

The first cat, Gelato, strides in, head upturned, tail straight as a ramrod, loud meow, indignant, assertive. Directed straight at me. Her presence fills the kitchen. I glare back, but my hand reaches for the door of my brand-new fridge just the same. I find it difficult to open this new fridge. I have to twist my wrist around the handle and not all my fingers fit properly.

Now, my old fridge, that was a different matter. You gave it a good heave, the deteriorated rubber gave a satisfying smack sound and the contents with all their cracked shelves and broken fixtures were revealed although, if it was night time, you had to switch on the kitchen light because the fridge light didn't work. And it was a fat fridge, not an anorexic one like this new thing.

I thought of my mother when I was a child having to cope with an ice chest. I remembered the way her singing would fill the kitchen space in the corrugated-iron shed we lived in as she busied around, her head over the old Primus stove, pumping and making it light with a whoosh. I sensed the drama of the operation at the time, but didn't realise how easily it could have blown her face off, or set fire to her hair.

When my old fridge finally packed it in, I had felt unexpectedly depressed. It had been part of my life for so many years it felt like part of the family. How many times had I reached up to the clock radio on top or to the old margarine container where I hid jewellery of sentimental value? The magnets on the front with endless streams of my children's drawings and photos, years of childhood memories and milestones. And the things that had fallen behind it. Cockroach baits, broken pens, dead flowers. Who knew what? Never to be recovered.

Its deterioration had been slow. First, the freezer door fell off, then the cover for the butter compartment. The thermostat controls gave up the ghost soon after and the magnetic strips and brand name clunked to the floor one morning. It leaked a bit and broke down at times. Marco, a retired Italian who knew about fridges, would come and breathe a bit more life into it. But the last time I rang, he'd gone back to Italy. Finally, the hinges of the door loosened and I had to use an elasticised bicycle strap to keep it closed. I'd hook one end to the door handle and the other to the side. (I see myself doing it as I read this years later and I want to cry, grieve for my young self and those hard times when there were not enough pennies to go around.) This worked well enough until the ants found they could slip through the crack and help themselves to whatever they fancied.

After I'd bought the new fridge, I'd emptied out the contents of the old one. It looked momentarily relieved of its burden. Fresh, years younger. I watched through the front window as the men came to take it away. It stood on the footpath staring back at me, denuded and abandoned. I turned away. Then a rattle, bang, crashing sound. I rushed back to the window and there was my old friend being ripped limb by limb. Door wrenched off, crushed and dismembered. Thrown into the waiting skip.

As I ladle the lumpy cat food into Gelato's bowl, her head goes into the dish immediately, even before all the food is in. She is also a glutton for comfort. Her heart seems to sing when she hears the first click of the gas heater going on, signalling the beginning of the cold winter ahead. The heater, a fairly thin, upright model, about half a metre tall with vents and a fan at the front, becomes Gelato's home for the coming months. She takes her annual leap onto the narrow, smooth surface at the top and simply lies there, stretched out for the duration. Because it's so narrow, her body overhangs, her rolls of furry fat spilling over the sides. Her tail has nowhere to go and simply hangs down the front. Why does she jump on top and not sit in front where the heat belts out? Because there is a gentle, never extinguished pilot light inside the heater which sends up an ascending shaft of delicious warmth, at just the right temperature, to luxuriously please her senses. Day and night.

If you chance to pick her up for a nurse, which she hates, her fur is warm to the touch.

So she lounges morning, daytime, evening. Even when I had to move all the lounge room furniture into the room with the heater because the floor in the other room was being sanded and polished, Gelato saw no reason to rearrange her day.

The room was chock-a-block full of tables, lounge chairs, cabinets and bookcases, even a queen-size mattress, but, with much craning, standing on tiptoes and pushing things to one side, you could just catch a glimpse of auburn fur, or the glint of a yellow eye, as she purred her way through the long hours of her life.

Book of Death

Selina was sacked from her waitressing job when she shouted at the chef for telling her how to arrange a sprig of parsley on a plate of steak and mushrooms. 'For crying out loud,' she screamed, throwing her apron in his face. 'You don't need a university degree to stick a few leaves on a plate. Get off my back and take your pathetic gripes somewhere else. The further the better.'

But it wasn't the job that was the trouble, that made her short-tempered and angry. It was her love life and the recent departure of Mervyn, her childhood sweetheart. It wasn't that Mervyn had fallen in love with another woman. No, he'd fallen in love with his computer. Or was it that he was trying to avoid Selina? Was he getting tired of her rants and raves about everything even the commercials on television? Early in the piece, Mervyn had insisted on watching non-commercial channels in a genuine effort to make things work.

But Selina never noticed or acknowledged his goodwill. Instead, she'd grab the remote and surf around until she found something to her liking. Quiz shows (she'd rant at the commercials) were her favourite even though she never knew the answers to the questions. In the process, she'd increase the volume until the combined effect of sound and the constant array of dumb contestants was to drive Mervyn further and further away until he was safely lounging in front of his screen in the spare room, toes wriggling in his Ugg boots, headphones firmly planted over his ears.

It was only a matter of time, Selina knew, before he'd inch towards and then rush out the front door with the rice cooker and soda stream he'd brought with him when he moved into her garden apartment six months earlier.

Selina was not sorry. She was fed up with her life. She needed to put some distance between the halfwits and idiots she was surrounded by and seek out new pastures. After she'd left school, her parents had insisted she learn to type and write shorthand so she could get an office job while she patiently waited to get married. It was what girls did.

She couldn't believe her luck when she landed a job as a secretary at the Australian National University in Canberra that included accommodation at a government hostel. As she shivered in the car park and unpacked her clothes in the tiny room, she realised she'd come to one of the coldest places in the country.

That first winter was bleak. She would force herself out of bed and before making her way down the corridor to the shared bathroom, flick on the switch of the electric radiator sitting in its usual place on the floor, closing the door behind her so the chill would be gone when she returned. But one morning when she came back, the room was as icy as the frost she could see on the roofs of the cars in the car park below her window. A typical Canberra winter morning, bare trees, sky the colour of aluminium.

The radiator obviously wasn't working. She picked it up. Held it in her two hands. She could see that the wire that wrapped around the element was broken. She could see the two loose ends. Her eyes were gritty, she was late for work. She was cold, tired, not sure what to do. Impulsively, without thinking, she reached in behind the safety guard with the idea of twisting the two ends together to get it going again. She had forgotten the heater was switched on.

Later, Selina wrote in her journal,

The bolt of electricity was instant, the impact throwing me backwards. The radiator came with me, stuck to my hands with the force of the 240 volts pumping through me. I could smell my burning flesh, the deadly current coursing through my upper body. My scream filled the air. I tried to yell again but the muscles around my lungs were paralysed.

It was then I had my near-death experience.

It was like I'd been split in two and a second, mirror image of me appeared out of nowhere. Detached, observing, confronting me. The second me was not taking any part in the proceedings, she was simply there. Impassive and untouchable. I had no time to linger on denial or incomprehension. There was no emotion, my thoughts came like hard hitting punches. This was no game, no practice at life and death. There would be no second chance. I had only lived twenty years, experienced five adult summers. It didn't matter, there would be no mercy.

People talk about seeing a white light, stepping outside their bodies, seeing angels. But I say, everyone's life is different. My life was unique. It flashed before my eyes, slowly. In colour. Not in a cinematic fashion, as I suspect many people would imagine. I saw a large, thick book with a dark cover. The book opened by itself and the pages began to flip over at an even and measured speed. The pages kept turning, then abruptly stopped. I couldn't understand. The book had just started, there were all the rest of the chapters to read. I waited for something to happen.

Then I realised nothing was going to happen. The choice was mine. What did I want? I could live or die. It was totally and utterly my choice. The other, outer me was still standing there, implacable and expressionless. There would be no help from her. There were only a few chapters of the book lived, the rest lying waiting depending on what I decided to do.

My leg flew up and with my slippered foot I kicked the radiator with all my adrenalin charged strength. It dropped to the floor. I gasped the oxygen into my lungs, my nostrils filling with the acrid smell of burning flesh. I was back in the real world, a terrified, wounded young girl.

I flung open the door and screamed my way towards help, on fire with fear.

Mervyn heard of the terrible accident Selina had after she walked out of her waitressing job and relocated to Canberra. Over a sprig of parsley, for heaven's sake. He felt sorry for her of course, but secretly couldn't help thinking it served her right to some extent. Her dangerous impulsiveness, strong-headedness, was always going to get her.

She was recovering at her parents' house when he visited, reclining on a sofa in her old bedroom with its teenage posters of Michael Jackson and Jennifer Lopez. In the corner was a dressing table with a framed oval mirror and assortment of boxes and bowls where she kept her earrings and bracelets. And next to her perfume bottles, a little bowl containing her rings. Large, chunky, teenage stuff.

But the thing that struck Mervyn was the array of black and white photos on the side wall of Selina's diving achievements beginning as a beaming thirteen-year-old scooping the winning medals at school athletic carnivals year after year, working her way up from the lower diving platform to the highest. Then finally at the age of just nineteen years winning the NSW Amateur High Diving Championship in 1968. The youngest on record. Mervyn remembered that day. He had been sitting in the grandstand as she'd stood proud and strong at the top of the diving tower before soaring forward, arms outstretched like angel's wings into a swan dive and straightening in a flash as she faultlessly pierced the tiny square of water below. She'd been a media star for months and even now her name was quoted by coaches and commentators at major swimming events.

They exchanged pleasantries like distant friends. Both were tongue-tied and in desperation Mervyn pointed to the array of diving photos.

'That takes guts. Nerves of steel. How did you do it? Calm your nerves? Leap into nothingness?'

'The trick is not to think. Just act. No use over-thinking these things, Mervyn.' Was she smirking at him?

Later that evening over his third schooner, Mervyn reflected on his visit. He couldn't fathom how any sane person could teeter on the tip of a diving platform ten metres above a patch of water about the size of a postage stamp and leap forward. Weren't we hard-wired to turn away from danger?

Selina's recovery was slow but eventually she emerged from her bedroom and resumed her job in Canberra. But something was not right. There was a cautiousness that wasn't there before. She felt cowed, slapped down. Beaten. There was no one she could talk to and soon her spirits sank and she teetered on depression. She thought back to her swimming days, how she had quickly graduated from laps of freestyle and butterfly to the diving board. That's when she had felt most alive. When her body was tingling with adrenalin and a fear that thrilled her even as it hovered and circled like a wild animal closing in on its prey. But she had stared the fear down. Beaten it. She wanted to feel that again.

At first, when she began swimming lessons as a young child, her coach had despaired of stopping her gazing upwards at the diving towers as she swam what to her were endless, meaningless laps. Eventually, her parents had relented and given permission for her to start diving lessons. And so she had climbed the ladder, literally. At first to the three-metre diving board, then five-metre and eventually to the very top, the ten-metre tower. She won multiple awards and trophies, culminating in the prized NSW Amateur High Diving Championship.

Selina's stomach tightened as she relived those days. She'd had no fear. No hesitation. But could she do it now? Her Canberra experience with the broken radiator had shaken her. She could have died. It had been touch and go. Those voices that had played in her head? Had they wanted her to live? Or die? Were they friendly or evil? And were they now responsible for the tumult and conflict in her head? Screaming at her that she'd lost her nerve.

She drove herself to the pool. She had thought of telling Mervyn but he was the last person who would understand. No, she'd face this alone. She selected locker No. 7, giving in to superstition that it was a lucky number, and shoved her towel inside. She left the key in the lock. She didn't know why.

She climbed the ladder, bypassing the lower boards, until she was at the top, a breathtaking ten metres above the pool, the equivalent of a three-storey building. The patch of chlorine blue water below looked like the size of a handkerchief. She inched to the end of the diving platform. A touch of vertigo hit her. Her toes tightened as if their grip would somehow keep her stuck in place. Without warning, just like the time in Canberra, her whole life flashed past her eyes. This time,

Mervyn was in the picture harassing her, waving his finger as if she was a naughty child. Even a few scenes from her favourite quiz show *Millionaire's Jackpot* slid past. Just like her Canberra experience, she saw twin images of herself. One thrashing around, tackling the world, dashing here and there. Blindly running from one thing to another. Listening to no one. And the other image watching and saying nothing. It was like she was split in two. One impulsive, the other passive. They were both beckoning her. Which should she follow?

Then, like her Canberra experience, the images stopped. There was silence except for the poundin of her heart. Her brain, her very self was blank. Frozen. Which one of her twin selves should she listen to? Which was her friend, which her enemy? She badly wanted to give into the fear racking her body and climb down the ladder. But without thinking it through – just like when she touched the radiator –she tipped forward on to her toes, swung her arms to shoulder height, lowered her head. And dived.

She'd cheated death before. Surely, she could do it again.

Step by Step

Jeremy dropped his train ticket on the seat of the train. It went halfway down the back. There was a blind man sitting opposite. What would he do if he dropped his ticket? Jeremy wondered. The blind man was a young man, with a beard. Well, more like a rough covering of hair. Was it hard for him to shave? Did he stand in front of a mirror? He was tall, quite lithe, wearing a white shirt unbuttoned at the neck, no tie. Black trousers. Briefcase. No dark glasses. A modern blind man. He had a big, warm, blonde Labrador strapped into a harness which he held onto through a metal lead. It led him to a seat. How did the dog know where there was a vacant one? Jeremy wondered again. The dog sat between the blind man's feet, the warmth and fullness of its body against each of the man's legs. Jeremy looked at the man's face but it was hard to read any expression. He felt embarrassed as if he shouldn't be looking, which was ridiculous considering the man couldn't see. Could he sense?

The blind man stood up as the train pulled into the station, giving the signal to the dog by giving a slight tug to the lead. 'Come on, let's go,' he said softly like two people who've known each other for a long time, comfortable and intimate. As he spoke, he ran his hand over the dog's coat, a long stroke which reassured them both. The dog stood.

Again, Jeremy looked at the man's face. What was going through his mind? Did he have to focus on the simple (to us) act of getting off a train to the exclusion of everything else? His chest suddenly seemed thin and vulnerable. Was he feeling fear? Jeremy thought of asking if he needed help, but he seemed so confident, independent.

There were a number of people standing in front of the doors also waiting to get off. The man put one foot firmly forward, the doors opened, the dog moved off and so did the man. At the time, Jeremy

"]

couldn't work out how he knew when to step over the gap from the train to the platform, but he did without hesitation. Afterwards, he thought perhaps the man knew the distance and knew each footstep had to be the same. How did he muster the courage each time? The dog led him.

The platform was crowded. No one took much notice of him, although many eyes went towards the cuddly dog with the big brown eyes. The two of them got to the flight of stairs which led to the ticket gates and which Jeremy went down every day to work. Jeremy was behind him and found himself tensing. Stairs? The man put one foot forward, again with confidence. The dog followed by his side. The man negotiated the first part of the steps, got to the landing and walked forward until he reached the next lot, and down he went again. Almost gliding. A sort of technique where he slightly bent his foot at the beginning of each stair to feel that it was a stair.

They got to the bottom and the man turned left and Jeremy went straight ahead. The last he saw of them was the upright figure of the man, arm outstretched to hold the dog's harness, striding forward and the dog trotting beside him, tail wagging furiously.

Thy Will Be Done

Donald O'Sullivan had an uncle called Mickey. Through a convoluted series of events, Mickey fled his home in New Zealand to take a job as a wharf labourer in the Sydney docksides. The family were as Irish as could be, and Catholic of course. Charm, humour. But also touched by the blarney that goes with it. No one could vouch for the family anecdotes repeated over the years but all agreed their humour and entertainment warranted the wee bits of flights of fancy and colouring around the edges that they came with. Donald's Irish-born mother could not be convinced that leprechauns were not real or that the shamrocks her sister sent from Ireland did not protect her from the Devil. A family anecdote often took on the whimsy of a fairy story.

So Donald couldn't vouch for the story of Mickey's sudden departure but this is what he was told: Mickey was staying with his brother Keiran in Winton, a small town on the South Island, when he rushed home one day and said he was booked on a ship bound for Sydney. He had been arrested for playing two-up and in the process had assaulted a policeman. If he didn't run away, he'd be arrested and go to jail. He gave his overcoat and spare clothes to his brother Keiran, telling him to sell off his other bits and pieces. Mickey jammed a few possessions into a rucksack and carefully wrapped his Bible and Rosary into the woollen scarf his mother had knitted him in the bitter winter of 1938.

A week later, Keiran was arrested walking up the main street of Winton wearing his brother's overcoat. Because of the strong family resemblance, the sergeant could not be convinced that he was not Mickey. Assaulting a policeman was a serious crime and the pressure was on to get the offender. If it hadn't been for the stern intervention of Father Joseph O'Reilly from the local Sacred Heart Catholic Church, Keiran might well have been charged. The police force was overbalanced with Catholics in those days, so admonishment from Father O'Reilly put more fear into the sergeant than any magistrate could have. After a nervous couple of hours, Keiran walked free, making a point of donning the overcoat and slowly buttoning the front.

In Sydney, Mickey got a job at the docks and found lodgings in the nearby sailor's home. He was older than the other men and had never finished school so had little choice but to shoulder the demanding physical work of unloading whatever cargo the swinging cranes dumped at his feet. Bags of raw sugar, wheat, flour, bales of wool or sacks of potatoes. He was not averse to ripping the hessian on the potatoes and taking a handful for boiling on the camp stove in his room later on. A mention in the Confession box and a few Hail Marys was all it took to salve his conscience. He might have a beer or two with his mates at the Fortune of War but mostly he applied himself to the life he was born to. Walking the path of a faithful Irish Catholic.

His first Christmas approached and after attending Holy Mass every day for two weeks, he felt the stirrings of homesickness. He belonged to a large Irish Catholic family and his faith and family were his core. He remembered that Keiran's son, Donald, had moved to Australia some years before. Had run off, actually. Things in the huge family with the small house had got to him. Donald had recently married and had a baby girl. Mickey managed to find out that Donald lived in Cootamundra and decided to take the train and pay him a visit. When Donald heard of his uncle's coming visit, he was somewhat taken aback and did not know how the meet-up would go. Donald had jumped on a ship when he was a teenager longing for another life but, more, longing to shake off the neglect and overcrowding that was his experience as a child growing up in a family of twelve children. He had had little contact with his family since then.

'But over a pint Mickey became quite sentimental,' Donald told a friend. 'Quite abruptly he offered me fifty pounds towards a deposit on a house. I was thrilled and we continued talking and ordering schooners well into the night. All went well until somehow the conversation turned and Mickey discovered my wife and I had married in the Church of England and not the Catholic church. It got worse when he learnt that not only that, our daughter, Helen, had not been christened Catholic, as was her birthright, he had said. I argued with him, telling him that I had to choose between the woman I loved who was a Protestant, or the church. Surely he could understand that I had chosen my wife? Wouldn't he have done the same?'

But just like that he withdrew his offer and rushed back to Sydney, where he quickly wrote an impassioned letter to his brother Keiran. The writing was scratchy with many crossings out and blotches. The spelling showed his lack of schooling. But the fury and outrage jumped off the page.

Waterside Federation
Sussex St, Sydney
Sept 1946

Dear Keiran

I am writing to you this letter much distressed. I do not know if all the family knows the scandal (sic) that Donald your Brother has brought on our family having married a protestant in a protestant church.

The next lines were heavily etched on the page as Mickey's fury escalated and he raged at Donald's child being christened Helen, with an 'H'. He took it as a direct insult to his beloved church. Every Irishman knew the correct Catholic name was Ellen. Even Donald's own mother was called Ellen.

You would think that he might have done it in haste but to go to the same church and have his innocent child baptised a protestant with that foreign name Helen. Note the letter H. He has no more write (sic) to take that innocent Child's Catholic heritage from her. You see what he has done with his Father's Name. I am longing for the day you meet him and ask him to put up his hands and defend how he has insulted you and your family. He was responsible for me spending the train fare to go there and shake hands with a traitor. He even made a fool of me. Got me to come up and see him. I have since regretted I did not give him a good hiding…

The letter trailed off as space on the page ran out. Keiran knew it would have been painful for Mickey to apply himself to the task of writing words on paper. The rush of semi-literate outpourings was a measure of the force of his feelings.

As the years rolled on, Mickey forged a life in his adopted country. Not so hard really, as he only had two loves. First and always, the Holy Catholic Church, and secondly, his beloved rugby union. He of course followed the mighty All Blacks of his homeland, a national sport in New Zealand and, although an undemonstrative man, found himself stamping his foot along with the giant players when they hammered out the Maori haka waving their angry tongues at the Wallabies, crashing their elbows across their chests. Masters of intimidation.

He made friends with a fork lift driver at the wharves, a fellow Kiwi from Otaki called Croppy Phelan, also a man of faith, who was as fanatical about rugby as Mickey. Every Saturday, they'd meet in Mickey's room in the seaman's home, where Mickey would make corned beef and pickle sandwiches and they'd make their way to the hill at the Sydney Cricket Ground. More often than not, it got ugly as fans, squatting on muddy grass, consumed cartons of beer and screamed at the players. One day, a woman in a blue sweater stood up in disgust. The man behind yelled at her to sit down. He couldn't see. She refused. Next thing, he hurled an orange straight into her back. Her friends rose in anger and next thing there was a full-on fist fight. When it was over, they all shook hands.

Afterwards, they'd catch a tram home, stopping for a few pints at the Fortune of War. Some would see this as boringly dull and repetitive, Mickey knew, but it suited him. He didn't like change or fuss and his two needs were satisfied on a weekly basis. Church and rugby. What was there to complain about? He found it difficult to keep in touch with his family in New Zealand. Phone calls were out of the question because of the cost and most of his family didn't have a telephone anyway. As for writing letters, Mickey would push the thought out of his head, not wanting to think of the treacherous Donald, who had fired him up to the point of picking up a pen.

Croppy Phelan was, by contrast to Mickey, an outgoing and sociable man. Never married, and Mickey never asked why. It turned out Croppy's family lived at Vaucluse, in Sydney's eastern suburbs. Mickey had never been there but knew it was called Millionaire's Row by blokes in the pub. Croppy never said much but it seems he'd turned his back on the family and been a runaway at school and disappeared for a year jackarooing on cattle stations around the state, only coming home when the money run out.

To his surprise, after about six months Croppy started producing free tickets to the matches. And not just a spot on the hill or in the stands but the best VIP seats in the grounds. Panoramic views of the field, free champagne and even the latest cocktails. Gin slings, mint juleps and white Russians.

As their friendship grew, Croppy explained that his father was a wealthy industrialist who owned a rubber factory at Balmain that manufactured tyres. He was a fair and just man. Indeed, a Christian. So, while Croppy was not exactly included in the family, his father had felt obliged to give him some sort of endowment. So he had recently passed down his lifetime private suite membership to the Sydney Cricket Ground to Croppy so he could watch his beloved rugby in style. This meant Mickey and Croppy happily lived in the lap of luxury for many years. No more the pathetic corned beef and pickle sandwiches. Now smoked mousse, olive and bacon skewers, devilled eggs and, Mickey's favourite, asparagus roll-ups.

Then the Lord in his unfathomable wisdom took a hand. A southerly buster was beginning to hit the city as Croppy walked towards a load of sheet metal about to be lowered on the wharf. A violent gust burst out of nowhere, caught the crane and tilted the load of sheet metal. Several sheets slipped and fell. Croppy was decapitated.

No one was more surprised than Mickey to learn Croppy had left him his private box membership in his will. He was just as surprised to learn that Croppy actually had a will. Apparently, it had been a condition of the gift from his father and Croppy, not having any other close friends, had bequeathed the membership to Mickey. Mickey was of course bereft at Croppy's death but another part of him which he kept to himself felt a thrill of pleasure at coming into ownership of such a priceless gift, unreachable to him in any other way.

Then July 1971 happened. The South African Springboks were coming to play the Wallabies. Mickey dreamed of the joy ahead picturing himself sipping French champagne in his private box. But instead all hell broke loose. Anti-apartheid protesters appeared everywhere, marching in the streets, disrupting games. A union official attempted to saw down the goalposts and a gigantic anti-apartheid effigy was hung from the Harbour Bridge.

The whole nation was in turmoil. Queensland declared a state of emergency. There were those who said sport should not mix with religion but commentators, politicians, union members and a huge slice of the population disagreed, were up in arms and would not have a bar of the match going ahead.

When Father Patrick O'Flaherty stood at the pulpit Sunday after Sunday and exhorted good Catholics to boycott the Springboks, stand up to the cruel racism of white South Africa, Mickey could no longer ignore the issue. He felt uneasy but was able to let the thunderous preaching slip off his shoulders after a day or two until Father O'Reilly finally spelt it out.

'Boycott the match,' he said, staring directly at Mickey. 'Stand strong like Our Saviour and take the blows and swords of thine enemies. Your brothers in Christ reach out to you. Do not turn your back on your coloured brothers. You, in your deep heart, must choose. Our Holiest Father, Pope Pius XII in Rome, has decreed that all Catholics must turn their backs on the evil this racist sporting event is perpetrating. Boycott the match. Your church? Or your rugby? It cannot be both.

Think. Pray. If you choose rugby, you will be spurning the Church and will not be welcome back into the fold. It will be permanent. No turning back. The doors to the heavenly kingdom will be closed.'

Mickey was torn to shreds. Never since that fateful day when he had discovered Donald had betrayed the church and married a Protestant had he faced such a moral issue. In that case, it had all been clear, black and white, he told himself. But this time? How could he relinquish his beloved rugby especially now he had lifetime membership to a private box? Hadn't the Lord himself been the one to bring that about? But, just as distressingly, how could he spurn his beloved church, the core of his very existence?

He wandered the streets and found himself outside the old stadium at Rushcutters Bay. He stood for a long time. He could hear the ghosts of the thousands of fans in the bleachers screaming with excitement and joy as their sporting heroes battled and forged their names into sporting history. The air was thick with the thrill of the match, the adoration.

He pulled his jacket close and turned slowly for home. He had made his decision.

Like Donald, he would choose the love of his life, rugby.

Truth Telling

My best friend Barb believes in the tarot cards. They guide her daily pathway and, most importantly, predict the future. In a nutshell, they are the truth. She places complete faith in their predictions and prophesies. Once they have spoken, her world is settled. She tells me they date back to the fifteenth century and are currently enjoying a renaissance in eastern countries.

But when she tells me she and her friend, Tillie, have taken them out to consult at this point in Barb's life when she is stricken with terminal illness, two tumours discovered in her body, in two vital organs, I feel uneasy and tense. What is Barb letting herself in for? But she is smiling.

'Of course, Tillie and I thought we must consult the cards.' She is beaming, jovial.

I don't like to ask outright, say the words, the words that are so hard not to skirt around. I hold my breath and feel my mouth tighten preparing to react appropriately to the oracle's answer.

But Barb hasn't asked the tarot cards about her dire medical condition. How serious? Would she recover? Or the big one, which I would have thought would be right up the oracle's alley, would she die?

But, no, she has asked them who would win the Melbourne Cup.

No Ticket Required But Watch Your Head

My father had a best friend called Doc Burns. They'd formed their friendship in the 1930s Depression when my father, at the age of twenty, arrived in Sydney from his runaway past in New Zealand. Doc was about ten years older and all I remember of him, when he visited us many years later, was his World War II army great coat, thick glasses and blotchy skin. There was some talk of a wife, but whatever it was, it hadn't worked out.

Although he and my father were sworn pacifists when they'd pedalled their bicycles around NSW, Doc was one of the first to enlist in the AIF when World War II broke out and one of the first Australian soldiers to be shipped off to fight in the Middle East to become one of the famous Rats of Tobruk. For eight long months, surrounded by German and Italian forces, he and his fellow soldiers in the Tobruk garrison in Libya withstood tank attacks, artillery barrages and daily bombings, enduring the desert's searing heat, bitterly cold nights and hellish dust storms. They lived in dugouts, caves and crevasses.

My father couldn't get over Doc's rush to enlist. 'We'd always sworn we'd never go and fight. We didn't believe in war or the capitalist powers that started them. We talked of joining the International Brigade to fight the Spanish Civil War and get rid of Franco.' My father would shake his head still puzzled to this day.

Before the war, Doc and my father had humped their blueys on foot and later on bicycles around the east coast of NSW looking for work and ready for adventure. In his memoirs, written not long before his death at the age of eighty-eight years, my father wrote, 'Doc showed me how to roll my clothes inside a blanket, drape them over the handlebars of my bike, sew up both ends and tie the whole thing to the frame. On our first night, we camped under a tree, I chopped wood for a baker in town and got a double loaf of bread. Doc weeded the butcher's garden and got some corned beef.'

Men in makeshift camps spent their time playing cards and making anything they thought they could sell – mothball containers, soap holders, toasting forks from scraps of wire, dustpans or candlestick holders from kerosene tins. Others whittled whip handles, walking sticks or props for clotheslines from the native bush timber.

My father and Doc heard they were employing day labourers in Canberra, where the rule was that you could camp at the showground for seven days but after that you had to leave. They had spent the night in Goulburn, a hundred kilometres away. Doc had a few days work cutting thistles on a nearby property so my father decided to meet him in Canberra. He would travel '4th class' on the Cooma mail steam train, which meant travelling for free on top of the train.

'I waited in the shadows of the Goulburn railway yards and darted out after the engine passed, still going slowly,' he told me. 'I managed to grab the rungs of the steel ladder on the side of the coal tender, and haul myself up to the bottom rung. You had to be careful because if you got caught, you could get beaten up by the railway guards. For some reason, even though they were workers, they'd give you a hiding, even using batons, if they found anyone trying to get a free ride. The steam train was picking up speed and I could feel my swag dragging my shoulder down as I slipped around on the bottom rung of the ladder. I thought I'd fall onto the track, in front of the wheels, but I managed to climb up to the roof of the train and hide on top with the lumps of coal. The driver and fireman were so close, I could hear bits of their conversation.

'As the train sped up, the trouble started. It was pitch-black. I was perched on top of the train. The air rushed past, the wheels clattered like mad and the engine lurched all over the place, threatening to pitch me over the side. Things started to settle down, but then I saw a black shape hurtling towards me. We were going flat out towards a tunnel and I didn't know whether I'd have my head chopped off. I screamed my fear into the blackness.'

His head was intact but he still had to survive two hours of cold, stinging water whipping across his face and sparks of coal flying around as the engine sped through the night. Eventually, he told me, the train reduced speed and he knew it must be getting close to Canberra station. He pulled himself up and climbed stiffly down the unsteady ladder, grasping the handrail of the carriage in front so he could swing free at the bottom.

'There was a woman sitting next to the window in the carriage as I swung past and she got the shock of her life to see a man's coal blackened face, wild-eyed and covered in soot, looking like he was coming through the door.' It was an image he never forgot. He was a polite man, always courteous to women and I thought that, even decades later, he felt bad that he hadn't been able to apologise, explain.

He jumped into the twilight, fell down the embankment, scrambled up, ran between the goods truck and hurled his swag over the high fence. 'I climbed over, jumped into a patch of weeds and onto a gravel road. My hand and elbow were stinging from gravel rash, but that was my only injury. I bolted as fast as I could.'

*

'Two hundred of us…angry, shouting men demanding justice… the whole atmosphere was vibrating with fear and violence. This was a moment of exaltation for me. No longer was I irrelevant and powerless. I was claiming what was mine and, right or wrong, I meant to have my voice heard…' Maurice O'Connor

The camping ground in Canberra for the unemployed men, my father told me, was a group of wooden barracks where men slept on the floor. They were not allowed to stay more than seven days. After that, the police would be around to make sure they packed their swags and moved on. 'But they did have hot water,' he added with a smile. 'After months of washing in creeks, dams and rivers, making sure no one was around, it was pretty good.'

He'd survived the trip on top of the steam train and he and Doc, who had arrived the night before, lined up for their seven days of work.

They couldn't believe their luck when they heard the government had decided to give two days extra work to everyone who was still there at Christmas, as a Christmas gift. 'It was a lot of money, two pounds instead of dole coupons worth only four shillings. The word got out and hundreds of people came to Canberra for the unexpected hand out. Swagmen. Bicycle bums. Train jumpers, and families in horse-drawn carts. The only problem was the seven days would expire before Christmas for the men already in the camp, including Doc and me. We'd miss out, kicked out on the road before we could get the extra pay.'

Years later, he recalled, 'There were two ring leaders in the camp. One was Hank, a tough Canadian lumberjack, and Darkie, a part-Islander who was wild, aggressive and dangerous once he'd had a few beers.' They called a meeting. My father was a compassionate man, his eyes still troubled as he went on to tell his story: 'Many of these men had been out of work for as long as five years. The humiliation and frustration they must have felt was ready to boil over. They appointed a delegation, headed by Hank and Darkie, to go and see the federal minister to ask for a week's extension so they could get the two extra days. The minister refused to see them. 'The men went to the local newspaper hoping for a sympathetic ear. Instead, the next day's headline read, "Bums Refuse to Accept Handout".'

My father's eyes blazed as he lived the moment again. 'The men decided to march en masse to the minister's office again and, if he didn't meet their demands, use sticks, stones or any other weapon they could find to break into the building. This time, the minister backed off and agreed to let us stay.' It was a pivotal moment for my father: 'But instead of feeling we'd won, I felt a sense of anticlimax, of being let down. I realised that the power had shifted from us back to the minister. He was the big man and we were once again the itinerants and mendicants, cowed down with a handout. We'd traded our stand for justice for a few nights' shelter.'

A few weeks later, he and Doc Burns went for a walk in nearby Queanbeyan. The lights were off to save electricity 'Without warning, a heavy blow landed on my ear. I swung to defend myself. Two large policemen stepped out of the shadows. "Get back to the camp, scum."'

The word had spread about the trouble in the camp. 'Next morning, when we lined up to get our two days' pay, they kept us waiting for two hours to teach us a lesson. A lot of things had happened to me since I'd been on the road. I'd been the fall guy in a boxing match to earn a few shillings, worked all day for a loaf of bread, even been stalked by a homosexual. But the behaviour of the Queanbeyan police was the thing that crossed the line. The camp disintegrated, drunken men fought or withdrew into themselves. Families simply vanished. Hank and Darkie, no longer having a common cause, turned on each other and out of sheer frustration fought and battered each other to a standstill,' my father recalled.

'The memory of those bloodied figures disappearing into separate huts after they could take no more always jolts me,' he said. 'They were the men who died a few years later in World War II, fighting for a way of life that had failed them so badly.

My father and Doc Burns remained firm friends but their lives went in different directions over the many years that followed. When Doc was terminally ill and my father, well into his seventies, wanted to pay one last visit to his old friend he told me, 'I walked into the hospital ward. There was an old man lying in one of the beds. We looked at each other. It was Doc, but we didn't recognise each other.'

Curly-haired Boy in a Fair Isle Jumper

There's a little girl called Merle standing in the playground of the small public school on the outskirts of Sydney, surrounded by other kindergarten kids. She's about five or six years old. The teachers are shuffling around, trying to get everyone into pairs. The children are going to do a peasant dance, swirl around.

Looking back years later, Merle can't remember much except that it started with the boy bowing at the girl and the girl curtseying. The teachers are running all over the place, perhaps they've drawn chalk circles on the bitumen. There's a lot of activity. Merle is swallowed up with shyness, not moving, not looking up. Will anyone ask her? Out of nowhere, a little boy comes up and asks to be her partner. He has short curly hair and is wearing a Fair Isle sleeveless jumper over his shirt. He's smiling. Merle is overcome by his sweetness. And not a little relieved that someone has chosen her.

His name was Reggie Enright and, a few years later, as soon as he could, he bought himself a motorbike, which was fairly common with young males as cars were far too expensive. He lived with his parents in a house near a railway crossing between Como and Jannali stations. The old ones, where a wooden pole lowered automatically when a train was coming, red lights flashed, bells clanged and cars waited for the train to pass. It could take ten minutes.

He was maybe fifteen or sixteen years old. His mother had asked him to go and buy her a packet of cigarettes. He got to the crossing only to find the barrier down, lights and bells activated. He knew the crossing better than anyone. He lived so close and was always going backwards and forwards. Plenty of time. He angled his bike around the end of the barrier, accelerated and headed for the other side.

The train rounded the corner. And he was killed instantly.

The tragedy was so great that eventually the railway station which was located further along the track near the railway bridge was relocated, holus-bolus to the site of the crossing. Gone were the boom gate, bells and red lights. And so was Reggie Enright.

His mother visited Merle's parents soon after. In between dragging on her cigarette, Reggie Enright's mother cried in agony. Racked with sorrow and guilt. Then the wailing commenced. Long and mournful. Over and over until she broke into a coughing spasm. Those damn cigarettes.

Early Memory of Impermanence

The tea towel is wet and soggy, limp and unpleasant in the girl's hand. She is about six or seven years old. Her eye level with her mother's rounded hip as her mother stands at the sink washing dishes in a chipped enamel basin. They are sharing a rented house at Como, an outer Sydney suburb, with the girl's aunt and family and the owner of the house, someone called Wagner. There is no hot water, so her mother has used the electric jug. When she finishes the dishes, the dirty water which has been used for everything from drinking glasses to greasy frying pans, will be hurled at the hydrangeas in the front garden.

The little drinking glasses with tiny patterns of daffodils and elves entrance the girl. Some blue, others yellow or orange. Neat circles around the rims. You got them when you bought jam or lemon butter. They were post-war cheapies, but her parents manage to turn them into pieces of magic by telling her sister and her fairy stories about the figures. Their father uses his imagination and humour to try to make up for the lack of money and material benefits he can provide. She wasn't sure it worked, but he did his best. For example, the girl and her sister never had dressing gowns. Instead, their mother would buy old men's overcoats from Paddy's markets, in Sydney's Chinatown, and although they felt heavy and rough on the skin, the girls felt like princesses wearing them and would parade up and down while their parents showered them with compliments.

How did they manage it, this conversion from old man's rags to a garment worn with glamour and pride? The sisters had been taken to a haberdashery shop earlier and allowed to choose a silky curtain cord with tassels in whatever colour they wanted. They were displayed on little hooks on the other side of the counter. Deep crimson, sapphire blue, sunset red, golden yellow, all luxurious and soft to touch. The cord was wound around the old man's overcoat with the tassels hung slinkily down the side transforming the ugly garments, in their eyes, into film-star magic. At night, the overcoats were thrown on their beds as extra blankets. Nice touch but they were threadbare and there was no warmth in them.

The girl can see her mother from her dwarfed position at the kitchen sink. She's sideways to the girl, head lowered, hands immersed in the flat suds. She has used the soap saver to get a lather, a small wire basket with a cake of Sunlight soap that she has whisked vigorously through the water. Her figure is rounded, an apron around her womanly waist. But the real apron string – the emotional one – can't be as easily untied and hung up on the hook behind the door. It's invisible, and maybe unbreakable, running from her centre core to the girl's, an umbilical cord that has never been broken.

The room around them is dark. No, maybe dingy is the right word. From nowhere, a wave of profound sadness sweeps over the girl, a sense of impending doom, though she is too young to know it as that. She becomes aware of loss, of the finality and pain that one day she will lose her mother and she will be gone, that there is no permanent perma-nence. The moment is so intense and frightening it is insurmountable.

The girl is so awash with misery, desolation, sadness, that it shows all over her face. Her mother asks the girl what is wrong. She doesn't answer but her heart is breaking. Her mother glances down at the girl, not seeing more than a petulant child. Perhaps she has problems of her own? Are her own everyday worries getting on top of her? The girl is hurt at her mother's off-handedness, locked up inside herself. She wants to grab her mother and hold onto her forever.

'Well, put the tea towel down and leave it,' she says. There is a tinge of impatience in her voice.

The girl puts the tea towel down and walks off, head down, body full of sorrow.

*

The feeling re-emerges many years later when the girl's mother is in hospital being wheeled off for an exploratory operation. The girl is now thirty-three years old. She leans against the doorway of the hospital ward as they take her mother to the operating theatre, her heart, her whole being silently with her mother on the bed. Every bit of the girl resists, screams to stop this happening, clings to the bond she feels with her, that old apron string just as strong as that day many years ago when her mother was washing up and the tea towel drooped in the girl's hand.

The nurses notice the girl's face. They try to cheer her up. It doesn't work, of course. She withdraws into herself as usual, and doesn't say anything. The exploratory operation discovers the worst. She has inoperable cancer. The apron string is pulling tight, will soon be ripped out of the girl. And she is not ready.

Not a Whisper From Me

Connie comes across the tiny locket unexpectedly. It's resting on greying cotton wool in a little heart-shaped blue box packed away with her childhood things. She sinks into a chair as the memories rush back.

It's a nine-carat gold perfectly shaped heart with soft rounded edges and decorative swirls. In the centre is a tiny sapphire-coloured stone. Her birthstone, September. She smiles remembering how people put a lot of emphasis on birthstones back then.

The locket has a little hinge. She opens it and inside there's just enough room to put a photograph or a lock of hair. A memory floats to her of her father snipping a curl from her head and placing it inside. But it's long since gone. She runs her fingers along the linked chain that holds the locket, surprised at how short it is. Made for a small neck. She smiles. Hers.

It would have been Christmas in 1952 when she was eight years old that she was given the gift. It must have been a good year because her parents had little money and the locket would have been a big expenditure. Gold, no less. She sees her father's beaming face. Her mother is there, too, but it's his joy that's coming through. He is bursting with happiness as he hands the little box to her.

Connie leans back in her seat, the memories swirling, as she relives the way she found out it was not real nine-carat gold. And not a real sapphire. The mean-minded boy next door had taken great delight reading the tiny writing on the back of the locket and telling her it was only one-tenth nine-carat gold. One-tenth? Whoever heard of such a thing? And the stone was probably glass, he had said.

She was shocked not so much for herself but at what it would do to her father if he knew what the boy had revealed. So she kept quiet and never told him. In this way, she never spoiled his joy of giving or hers of receiving this little bit of treasure that, to her, was pure gold.

That mean-minded boy was called Patrick. He liked to show off and make things up. Like the time he boasted that he'd found a pipe under his house and, if he put his ear to it, he could hear his parents talking upstairs. When he was about seventeen years old, he got a job working in the city. He had to travel each way by train and in those days the train doors did not close automatically so, if you wanted to, you could leave them wide open and watch the tracks flying past. It was the cool thing to do. They said Patrick had been standing too close to the edge. He had fallen off and an oncoming train ran over him. His leg was so badly mangled, they had to cut it off.

Saturday Morning in a Country Town

There's a man slowly walking down the main street of Lithgow on a cold, busy Saturday shopping morning. The year is 1945. He wears a dark suit, waistcoat, watch and chain. Large shoes, feet spreading like inkspots on blotting paper. Despite a slight stoop, he has a certain bearing as he ambles along, one hand on the pipe in his mouth.

You couldn't say he looks distinguished, certainly not sophisticated, but there is something a bit different. A sort of importance. But it's borderline, and could just as easily slip into ordinariness and make him the same as any of the battlers bustling in the street. People notice him and have no reservations shaking his hand, saying 'g'day', cracking a joke maybe. There's a slight ripple of interest as he strolls along unaccompanied by any officials or companions.

Lithgow, in western NSW, is a workers' town surviving on the sweat and grind of railway men, coal miners and iron workers who have little in the way of industrial rights and still less in the way of money. It lies in the dip of a valley collecting mist and frost most of the year. The cold is bitter and, in a country of sun and desert, it sometimes snows.

There's also the small arms factory, where men churn out guns and rifles when Australia is in the grip of wars. Its history is grim. During World War I, over 1,500 men were employed producing 20,000 rifles and bayonets a year. The town sank under the unexpected influx; there was no sewerage, roads were dirt tracks and there were simply not enough beds. People resorted to overcrowded and sometimes condemned houses, tents and even crude humpies. Then, when the big guns stopped and the war was over, the town suffered a massive slump as the biggest employer in town turned off its machines. There was an attempt at making other things – car parts, shearing sets, and even golf clubs and artificial limbs – but nothing equalled the profits of war and the number of jobs dropped to a mere three hundred.

But that all changed in 1939, when World War II broke out. A mixed blessing. While some men caught the steam train to Sydney to enlist, others – including Walter's father – were deemed by the government to be essential manpower and found themselves punching the Bundy clock at the factory.

Accommodation burst at the seams for a second time as the factory looked for 6,000 men, this time to produce around 200,000 British Lee-Enfield rifles. Air raid shelters had been built a few years before, following the Japanese submarines entering Sydney harbour in 1942, windows blacked out, sirens installed and mighty 3.7-inch guns erected at either end of the Lithgow valley.

The men at the factory, Walter's father included, work by bells. The first rings out across the town's corrugated-iron rooftops, with their layers of coal dust, at six a.m., making sure the workers wake up. The next, an hour later, is to tell them to line up on the factory floor at their machines. Five minutes later, a supervisor sitting in a room above throws a master switch and simultaneously the rows of machines surge with electricity, the men standing to attention next to them, ready to move. Two minutes later, the last bell clangs and the men lean into their work benches on the production line and the factory is filled with the deafening sound of metal on metal. They work twelve-hour shifts and sometimes a doubler, or even a tripler. They are as mechanised as the machines, repetitiously punching the same conveyor belt and pulling the same levers. No skill required. Communism is getting a look in.

It's the usual Saturday morning shopping scene as the lone man strolls along the grey street. Everything shuts at twelve noon, so there's not much time for people to do their business. A bit of traffic but it's never a bother in a small town like Lithgow even in the main street. Women wear drab hats and carry string bags for their groceries. There are no supermarkets, everyone goes to the Co-op. It started at the turn of the century as a way of saving money by getting rid of the middleman. People get a share of the profits, not by how many shares they've bought, but by how much money they spend. At first, it simply baked cheap bread but soon grew and now trades in everything from food and livestock to clothes, hairdressing, dentistry and even funeral and black-smith services. The birth of supermarkets, some twenty years in the future, would eventually kill off the Co-op but no one knows that now.

People window-shop at places like Manfolds, Bracey's, Suttons Butchery & Bakery and, of course, most of the men will end the day at the Lithgow Workers' Club, set up in someone's house in 1887 by a handful of thirsty railway men and coal miners who had no time for licensing laws. It soon became the watering hole for workers weary after a long shift and hungry for a bit of cheer as the long frosty nights settled around them. As time passed and numbers swelled, it shifted to an empty hall near the railway line and now, thanks to the blind eye of the local copper, keeps its doors open around the clock.

The centre of activity seems to be the chocolate wheel set up every Saturday to raise money for the local hospital. Someone calls out to the dark suited man, 'Come on, mate, have a go.' People gather around, a bit of excitement on a frosty morning. 'Ya never know your luck, give it a go.'

The man is not known for spending money lightly, even the zack (sixpence) needed to buy a ticket on the wheel. He digs into his pocket, however, and comes up with the coin. The wheel is spun, flies around rapidly until the flap starts bouncing against the last metal prongs. It loses momentum and stops on a number. The man is surprised to see he's won.

The prize is a huge cooked ham weighing about eight pounds (four kilograms). He reaches out and takes hold of the thick string looped through the top of the lump of meat. It's heavy and his shoulder drops momentarily as he takes the weight. A tiny smile strays across his lips as he turns and continues his amble up the main street, happily swinging his bounty beside him.

'I always thought it was a strange thing to see,' Walter's father told him years later. 'There was Ben Chifley, the prime minister of Australia, and the local member for Lithgow who'd come for a visit, strolling along the street with a great lump of ham swinging on a bit of string from his arm.'

Schoolkids

I'm sitting inside at my desk.

Out of the quiet suburban blue comes the distant exuberant sounds of young children laughing, talking, feet pounding excitedly down the footpath.

The crocodile of kids gets louder, snatches of words, yelps, giggles, laughter. Some voices louder than others, more mature, but all childish right outside the front of my place.

The energy flows in through the open door and windows. A few stragglers. An adult voice at the end.

'Stop at the next corner,' the teacher calls out, as the kids from Cammeray public school rush past my house, down the street, to the park below for their sports day.

I can see my darling son Anthony, long legs, short pants, bounding along amongst them, excitedly telling everyone, 'That's where I live.'

Suddenly there's silence. They've gone. They've moved on.

Starchy's Dream Ending

I'd hated Starchy since we were kids fighting over empty bottles behind the pub in Wilson Street, up the road from Eveleigh railway workshops where my old man worked twelve-hour shifts in the locomotive sheds. You could get a zack a dozen from the bottle-o, so we were always kicking and shoving each other to grab as many as we could. He came at me once with a broken long neck and that put the wind up me. Nicked me on the leg before I could run away. I knew then he was one to watch.

Even sitting next to me at St Benedict's school, he got on my gander. Especially with his stupid, lopsided face. Mouth like a fish hook. I heard my mother and Mrs Kilkerry gossiping over the fence about Starchy's mother. Saying she'd been attacked when she was a girl by her uncle who'd got her pregnant.

'And worse still,' Mrs Kilkerry's voice had dropped to a whisper and I'd had to lean in to catch her words, 'the Lord punished her for her sins. The baby came out with such an unholy cry that his mouth was twisted so badly it never came right again.'

My mother had sat back in her chair frowning.

'Believe me, Maureen, it was the Lord who put his mark on the boy to show everyone the punishment that awaits sinners like her. A mark Starchy will have for life.'

My mother stood up with such force her chair toppled backwards. 'Holy Mother of God. And what about the uncle? What about the miserable coward? What was his punishment?'

*

There was a time when my father dreamt he might escape the drudgery of the sheds with his singing. Everyone said he could carry a tune. He'd start up in the pub after his shift and the men would shout for more. When they started calling him Velvet Voice, he shot up about six inches. He learnt the words of all the pop songs. 'Meet me in St Louis, Louis', 'When Irish Eyes are Smiling' and his favourite, 'In My Merry Oldsmobile'.

He'd stand in front of the dingy mirror in the washhouse practising his smile, flashing his eyes and squaring his jaw. His big break came when he entered the Salvation Army talent quest. You could do all sorts of things. Juggling, tap dancing, whistling, play the accordion. Even make bird calls with a gum leaf. He picked the new jazz number to show how modern he was. 'Bill Bailey Won't You Please Come Home'. When they told him he'd won first prize, he knew heaven had dropped into his lap. It wasn't the twenty quid prize, but the unending horizon he saw opening.

Who knows what might have happened if there'd been no war? Just two years after his hope of getting out of a life at the sheds seemed within his reach, World War 1 broke out and before you could say Jack Robinson he was a soldier in khaki marching off to Egypt to help the bloody Poms beat the Germans. By the time he got home, his singing days were gone. The country was flat as a tack. Jobs were scarce as hen's teeth and the last thing anyone wanted was a singer. Because he was a returned Digger, they took him back at the sheds but anyone could see the stuffing had been knocked out of him.

*

A part of me felt sorry for Starchy being born on the wrong side of the blanket and having a mother who was a sinner. But what happened next changed that forever.

It was the usual Saturday matinee at the Empire Picture Theatre in Enmore. The routine was always the same. Starchy would push his way into a seat next to me, yelling and screaming when the Indians butchered the cowboys with their tomahawks. He even yelled and laughed when the horses went down. I would shout at him to shut up and pull his head in. Most of the time, he'd drop back in his seat and keep quiet. But one Saturday he didn't.

He moved closer to me until he was pushing against my leg, yelling and making faces. He twisted towards the screen, laughing as the Indians circled the wagons and arrows and rifles went off left, right and centre. He slipped his hand down the front of his trousers and I could see him fumbling with the buttons on his fly. I felt sick. Don't tell me he's a bloody faggot as well.

Things happened fast. Starchy seemed to fall towards me, grinning and spluttering with laughter, eyes full of madness. I tried to get up from my seat to push him back but he reached out and held me close for a few sickening moments. I could feel his stupid prick against me.

'Stop horsing around, you mug. Get away, you dirty faggot.'

I took a swing at him but he swerved away and laughing and screaming his head off, shuffled along the row like one of the Indians had jumped off the screen and was chasing him. When he reached the aisle, he ran off for all his worth, straight out of the theatre.

It was then I felt the warm, stinking liquid trickling down the front of my trousers, inside my bare leg and down to my socks and I realised Starchy had pissed on me. The sheilas in the row behind thought it was hilarious. And I copped it from my old man. He dragged me out to the dunnie.

'That's where ya go, stupid,' he screamed, pushing my head within an inch of the splintered lid.

After that, it was war between Starchy and me. He tried to sweet talk my sister, Eila, to get at me. I hated her, but that didn't stop me spying on them at the back of the oval. When he shoved his hand up her dress, I let fly with a brick to scare him. But next thing they were engaged. I knew it was to get at me.

*

Starchy and I were kicked out of school when we were twelve years old. Everyone knew Starchy was not the full quid, slow on the uptake, a dumbbell. We mucked around together, not because we'd stopped hating each other, but what could you do on your own? We nicked a couple of bikes once from the Protestant kids up the road and spent a day in

Redfern Park weaving around the alcos. We took turns swooping down and grabbing their sherry flagons. Geez, some of those old buggers could hang on tight. I'd circle around a few times then drop the bottles back. Poor old geezers, they'd die without their booze. But Starchy would pedal like mad to the back of the Moreton Bay figs, where he'd smash his bottles as hard as we could onto the graffiti on the wall of the toilet block. I can still hear him laughing like a maniac. Even I thought that was pretty crook.

It was 1921. We were Redfern kids and knew we'd end up, like our fathers, shut up for twelve-hour shifts under the stinking iron roof of Eveleigh. It was our fate. Some blokes ended up cot cases after a few years cleaning the smoke boxes or going deaf firing off rivet guns all day in the boiler room. All they got was a couple of bits of cotton wool to stick in their ears.

Then there were the poor buggers who worked in the hell hole of the foundry who had to put up with getting burnt by splashes of molten metal. Men came off their twelve-hour shifts covered in grease and soot, coughing and spitting up steel flakes, smelling of iron and sweat. They'd trudge up the hill to their drab terrace houses, pathetic shacks stuck together like flypaper, to booze the despair of the day away. If they were lucky, their missus might have a bit of corned beef, even underground mutton (rabbit, to the toffs). More than likely, though, it would be soup and rice pudding.

There were no showers, not even a decent tap. 'You'll be on the veranda tonight,' Starchy's old man would say to his mate, Hughie. 'The missus won't want you warming the bed.' It was a tired old joke, an attempt to regain lost dignity.

The sheds were like caves with ten-inch-thick sandstone walls and a roof that practically touched the sky. You could see a row of poky windows around the top which were supposed to let in light. What a joke. The only thing that got in were pigeons that flapped around like mad and, if they got lucky, found their way out.

From the minute the place opened, there were accidents. Men got crushed between locos in the dark, noisy sheds. In the machine shop, the conveyor belts that fed into the grinders were a constant menace. The belts moved fast and blokes got their fingers and hands crushed all the time. Old Eric tripped one day and landed head first on the belt. It moved so fast he couldn't get up in time and – crunch – his shoulder hit the grinder. He was lucky. They grabbed him before the rest of him went in.

*

Over the years, the cracks in Starchy's sick head got bigger until they were gaping so much you could practically see through them. He swore everyone was against him.

For instance, there was an old codger, Percy, who'd worked in the sheds all his life. Percy was a bookmaker and the year before, Starchy told everyone he was putting his life's savings on an outsider at Randwick. The nag came home and Starchy must have seen the road to riches gloriously unfold before him. But when he went to collect his winnings, Percy said the book had been closed when he tried to place his bet.

'Ya get nothing, kid. Ya never gave me yer money. Shake a leg next time and be a bit quicker.'

Starchy blew his stack, swearing and calling old Percy everything under the sun. He had it in his crazy head that Percy had welshed on him and pocketed the money. Everyone knew that was baloney but I saw another bit of blackness slip through one of the cracks and lodge itself in Starchy's miserable head.

Smoko was outside the grinding shop. It had a sign saying Ambulance Square but the union had taken it over as a rallying spot years ago, during the Great Strike of 1917, and renamed it Red Square. The strike was still fresh in the men's minds. It had started because the bosses wanted to bring in some Yankee idea of time and motion. Every bloke would have a card and the bosses would write down everything they did and how long it took. Even the canteen staff.

'Gawd blimey. How do you measure how long it takes to put a pie in the oven?' his father had bellowed.

The strike had spread from Eveleigh across the state. An engine driver at Bathurst, Ben Chifley, had taken up the fight and gone hammer and tongs for the workers' rights, but jeez, he'd paid the price. The strike lasted six weeks until the bosses found scabs from the bush and then they said, 'OK, you blokes come back to work, or get sacked.'

Chifley was told he had no job, then they gave in and took him back, but he was put down from being an engine driver to a fireman. That week the union stuck up a plaque in Red Square:

On this site the men of Eveleigh railway yards struck a blow for workers' rights. We stood up for a fair go and the one who stood tallest was an engine driver from Bathurst, Ben Chifley. A leader of men.

But the bosses ripped it down the next day. Little did they know Chifley would have the last laugh. He went on to be Australia's post-war prime minister.

There was a monster steam engine at Eveleigh called Buffalo a cast iron giant weighing two hundred tons. Big and brutal. The great barrel engine throbbed as steam hissed and spat through the firebox. Heat from the raw flames was intense. Men dripped with greasy sweat. The air stank of iron and acid. There was to be an official unveiling of Buffalo in a couple of days. The premier. Photographers. Reporters.

The pressure was on. Extra shifts were put on to finish the casings. Even Starchy, who was usually the last to get overtime, was told to hop up. The foreman yelled at us to get cracking and roll Buffalo onto the revolving turntable so men could work on all sides at the same time. Buffalo slid into place and the foreman rushed around, bolting it down at the rear. What? Only one anchor point? There was supposed to be four. What did the foreman think he was doing? Jeez, the heat must be on.

Percy, the old bloke Starchy was convinced had robbed him, had finished his shift and was walking away from the blasting oven towards old Buffalo on his way to the door. That's when I saw Starchy sidle up to the safety gate. He was trying to shield the lock with his back but I knew he was releasing it. Our eyes met and the hatred of our old days back in the pictures pierced the air between us.

Just when Percy would have seen the loco closing in on him, Starchy yelled over the din. 'Hey, Perce, give us a fag.' He waved his empty tobacco bag. 'Over here. See, it's empty.'

Just as Percy turned to look at Starchy carrying on like a madman, Buffalo picked up momentum and glided straight at the old man. Wham. That was it. Half his right side was smashed and anyone could see he wasn't going anywhere in a hurry except to the old Rum Hospital up the road.

'Crushed like a matchstick,' Starchy had told the cops later, throwing his arms high to emphasise the size and might of the loco. 'Nothing anyone could do. The engine charged clean through the safety gate. Just like a buffalo!'

He was the only one laughing. He knew I'd seen him slip the safety lock so I kept my distance. He didn't want me spilling the beans to the cops or, worse, letting the blokes know what I'd seen.

Accidents happened all the time at Eveleigh. Blokes had had fingers and hands crushed on the two-hundred-foot conveyor belt in the running shed before, so what was new? I hated having to work on it almost as much as I hated Starchy. You were so close to the bloke next to you, you practically touched, and you weren't allowed to talk, which didn't matter as the noise was like permanent thunder in your ears. But, this day, the foreman told me I had no choice, it was my turn.

I was pretty alarmed when Starchy grabbed a spot next to me. He had that stupid grin on his face and every time we swung the coils onto the belt and saw them speed towards the grinder, I felt his sweaty shoulder press against me, trying to throw me off balance. He wanted to heave me onto the conveyor belt, see me disappear into the grinder. Goodbye eyewitness.

So what did I do? Pushed back of course. We kept it up all morning until the siren went for smoko. Blokes rushed off and I saw my chance.

Starchy and I were the only ones standing next to the speeding belt. Our eyes locked and I knew it was either him or me. I swung my arm around Starchy's thick neck, kicked the back of his knees so he fell forward onto the moving belt. His head hit the rubber and before you could blink, he'd hit the grinder. His scream sent the pigeons into a frenzy. He didn't die but his scalp got ripped off his head just like the Indians in the cowboy pictures Starchy and I had watched as kids.

He always liked that part best.

Fairyland in the Bush

It must have been Christmas. No, it wasn't, it was Easter.

Behind the corrugated-tin shed my father built for us to live in while he built our house on the outskirts of Sydney was a huge slab of rock. It soaked up the sun during the day and I loved its warmth on my bare feet. I was about six years old.

As I look back all these decades later, I still remember the feeling of great mystery and wonder in the air that day. My father said he'd seen fairies living on the rock. My eyes popped. My mother would have been silently smiling in the background, her face framed in loose blonde curls, helped along with a Which Twin Has the Tony? home perm.

Down we went, quietly. And there they were. Little houses made of bright, moist green moss and tiny bits of rock. There were trees made of twigs and a few petals of lantana for the garden beds. They had front doors and pathways of sand. My sister Helen and I tiptoed and whispered our way around them, peeping inside, our imaginations running wild with images of winged magic. Our father was bursting with excitement and joy. He'd obviously been down there a day or so earlier and built our little fairyland. We were entranced.

I have no recollection of getting any Easter eggs (we probably didn't) but I never forgot the magic of that rock and kept believing in the fairies long after I should have stopped.

*

Another time, as my mind wanders back, I see kookaburras perched on the paling fence on the side of the house giving forth their fat man's belly laugh. My sister and I are sitting at the front of the house where my father has planted cuttings of buffalo grass in the hope they will spread and form a lawn. He is somewhere in the background, up a ladder, sawing something, wheelbarrowing a load of second-hand bricks my mother had cleaned with a trowel during the week while he was at work. He's wearing shorts, but no shirt because of the heat. Perspiration glistens on his chest but he always wore a shirt to sit down for lunch. A sign of working-class gentility back then.

He's got a leather bag around his waist with pockets and spaces for all sorts of tools, including a flattened pencil used by carpenters. He'd either have his old army hat on or a hankie tied at each corner to form a covering for his head. There would have been bits of things around, a wooden horse used for sawing timber. We were often called to 'hold the end' while he sawed or screwed, holding the nails between his teeth. He was always busy, always working, building or fixing something. If something broke or didn't work, Helen and I simply gave it to him to fix. From earrings to complicated mechanical repairs.

It was the era of the do-it-yourself man born out of post-Depression days when materials and money were short. He hadn't had any training in a trade but it turned out he had a good brain, worked things out and had a go. There's a lovely black and white photo of the day the framework of the house he was building was pushed into place. Standing tall, but naked like a skeleton. A long ladder leads up to the rafters on the roof, and there he is standing atop.

But it's the next photo that amazes me. It shows my sister and me also standing by ourselves on the top of the house, our hands neatly in front, big smiles. Nothing to hold onto and if we'd stepped backwards or forwards we'd have fallen to the ground. We must be at least fourteen feet (over four metres) from the ground. We'd obviously been encouraged to climb the wooden ladder and step onto the raw wood.

Back then, when the kookas were sitting on the fence, maybe my sister and I were pestering him for something, maybe we were saying we had nothing to do.

'Look. See the kookaburras?' The perspiration was glistening on his body and he kept working as he spoke. 'See how they laugh? Just keep walking past and pretend to fall over. That'll make them laugh.'

We tried for ages, getting up and falling over and over in every way we could think.

'Don't look at them.' My father looked up from nailing some floor joists. 'They'll know you're just pretending.'

The birds sat implacably, totally unamused. Not the slightest sound. Eventually, they flew away without so much as a chortle, no doubt as bored as we were.

Visit to Malcolm's Father

She found it difficult to get her thoughts straight after the bushwalk, climbing the hills and gorges around the rocky fringes of Sydney. One minute she'd been gazing at pink and gold-tipped wildflowers dotted along the rocky track and the next driving through the backblocks of the retirement village with her ex-lover Malcolm, to the end-of-the-line accommodation where residents progressed no further. Not in the living world anyway.

They entered the institutional expanse of sprawling villas through curved black iron gates that looked sad and forlorn, rather than grandiose and stately as the splashy brochures had promised when the developer put them on the market. The five-kilometre speed signs, in super-large letters, made sure they crawled along at a snail's pace, through the married couples' quarters to the outlying regions, which looked as grey and flat as the few hairs left on the heads of the residents. What a contrast to the shimmering light and colour of the bushwalk. Even the sky had faded to aluminium grey.

She'd been there twice before in her work as a journalist. Once was to interview a World War I veteran who'd become angry and impatient when she couldn't follow his story, obviously relived so much in his mind that he couldn't slow down enough to allow a younger generation listener to understand. A disturbing and unsatisfactory experience for both of them.

The other had been to interview that poor wretched famous swimmer, then in her nineties. They'd dressed her up, even a bit of lipstick, and put a soft pink rug over her old legs. Those shapely, strong, record-breaking swimming legs now needed the help of a wheelchair to get her around. Rather ironic that the swimming club was about to commemorate her with a delicately carved statue of a legless mermaid, placed on the headland overlooking the beach she had made famous. They said she'd been a bit of a wild thing in her day, the first woman to bodysurf in Australia. She'd had affairs with half the surf club, in the days when women didn't have affairs, let alone en masse, they said. She had searched the wizened face trying to gaze beyond her eyes to find a trace of the young, fiery, sexually active twenty-year-old. She drew a blank. Another disturbing and unsatisfactory experience.

She stared out the window of Malcolm's car, feeling herself slipping into the half-speed world of the place as they travelled further into the nether reaches of that red-brick-and-tile world of the very old. It seemed to take an inordinate time to drive through the 'old soldiers village' section to the backblocks where the beyond hope people were.

'He's finished, you know,' said Malcolm, referring to his father.

She felt apprehensive. She hadn't had any say in whether she wanted to go or not. She'd accepted a lift home with Malcolm at the end of the bushwalk and on the way he'd said, 'You don't mind if I drop in and see my father, do you? We have to go past the place.'

OK, they'd been lovers many years ago but they had decided independently to try to forget it had ever happened. Did that give him the right to include her in this dutiful visit? She felt uneasy. Tricked.

They resorted to small talk as they walked up the driveway through the swinging frosted doors into the foyer. She was in zombie mode both from adjusting to having come too quickly from the beautiful, living, limitless space of the outdoors and from attempting to block out the images and thoughts confronting her. This was death row but noone had committed an offence, except to get to the end of their lives.

They entered the tiny, canary-yellow lift. There were four others inside, so they were squeezed together. There was no privacy in a place like this, so she supposed it didn't really matter or seem unusually close. People's bodies and emotions were stripped bare pretty quickly inside these walls.

The other four were a family. Two terribly old people, one a resident, the other his wife, and two from the generation after. The man's son, she guessed, and his young wife, come for their obligatory visit.

She wasn't prepared for the sparks that flew. The short, acerbic words spat out by both the younger man and the old, crippled father. ('He's a doctor, you know,' she heard the old man tell the nurse later after they'd gone, still with pride despite the rawness.) It was only a couple of floors but a lifetime of some festering hostility was let loose. Over what? She didn't understand. As she stepped out of the lift, she caught the final words and realised they'd been feuding over a mistake in the visiting hours, for God's sake.

Trying to shake off the angst that had swirled in the lift, she and Malcolm stepped into the long corridor that stretched before them with its bright blue extra-shiny linoleum. The walls were white, with a smooth wooden handrail running along at waist height so wheelchair residents could steer themselves up and down the length of the dead end road, turn, and come back again. It was the only place they had to go.

Malcolm found his father sitting in his wheelchair, waiting for someone to take him for a spin down the confines of the corridor. Malcolm started pushing the unfamiliar weight, talking all the while as if he was the father and the broken man in the wheelchair the child. He stopped and there was an awkward pause when no one knew what to do, so she took over and zipped Les up and down another couple of times. He smiled as he skimmed his hand along the surface of the wall remembering what it felt like as a child running a stick along the bricks of a favourite building.

He spied the red button outside the entrance to each ward and as it offered the only mental stimulation he'd get all day, he pulled his wheelchair to a halt at each one and gave it a good press. He was dribbling at first. His body was sunken and his striped flannel pyjamas had the suggestion of a stain between his legs which looked like it was there for good, although someone had dressed him in a nice sporty pullover. His eyes were out of it, seeing their own dreams and demons. There were bristles on his chin and hairs on the end of his nose.

They weren't the only ones on the move. The whole floor was teaming with soundless activity, or perhaps it was more like wriggling. Men's bodies of all shapes and sizes were lying, sitting in shadowy corners in leather chairs or pulled up stationary in wheelchairs staring at nothing, going nowhere. One or two shuffled along in walking frames. All men, except for the nurses.

'What's your son's name, Les?' one asked Malcolm's father.

He hesitated and concentrated with all his might. She found herself tense wondering whether he'd know. To ease the situation she glanced at the signs around the wall.

'Give someone love, and you will receive love'.

'I need to know you love me, I need you to show me you love me'.

Suddenly, without too much delay or searching through his old brain, Les sang out his son's name and they all breathed a sigh of relief.

She gave Malcolm's father another ride and they found themselves at the entrance to the TV room. All she could see were colourless lumps of bodies arranged around the walls in an array of dark brown seats with grey blankets over their knees, no air, curtains drawn as the handsome game show young man spun his Wheel of Fortune.

It was too much for her and she couldn't bring herself to go on through the door. Fortunately, nor could Les. He held onto the sides of the doorframe as she pushed the wheelchair towards the entrance, using every bit of strength he could muster to stop the wheelchair from passing through. Thank you, Les.

The time came to leave and Malcolm said goodbye to his father. She kissed him on the cheek, twice. He smiled.

'You'll never get anyone as good as Malcolm,' he said, mistaking her relationship with his son who had just divorced his third wife and whose fourth wife she had no intention of becoming. 'See you later, potato,' Les said. His smile broadened at his wit, kept getting wider, filled his eyes, his face wrinkled, it kept going, then suddenly it had gone too far. He broke down and collapsed into tears.

On the way out, she stood at the lift waiting for the doors to open.

She could see the whole length of the blue and white corridor. There was a whole bank of them, a whole row of old, frail, deformed, sick men lined up one behind the other in their wheelchairs, like the carriages of a train, derailed up a side track. Just sitting, waiting.

'That's what you call a dead end,' her mouth tensed at her black humour.

They went down in the same bright yellow lift. This time there was no one else in it. Malcolm pointed to the lift buttons.

'The STOP button is really the GO button,' he said. 'It fools the patients.'

Lakes and Alps

Stefan drove down the main street of Taupo, a touristy town in the middle of the North Island of New Zealand, in his red open-topped car. I was in the front seat and Veronica, hair out of control and nose out of joint, in the back. We'd spent the previous night in an old Forestry hut after the weather turned so bad that Stefan decided a detour was advisable.

The huge expanse of Lake Taupo, for which the town is famous, was ahead, getting closer. I glanced sideways across the seat of the car and snuck a look at Stefan. He was excited, eyes intent, profile handsome. In control of the situation. Adrenalin just right. We'd only just met but the electricity snapped across the seat.

The road was straight and I could see a boat ramp in the distance. Stefan kept his foot on the accelerator and the ramp was steadily getting closer and closer. But still he kept going. People on either side of the road began to notice. They were curious, then startled, then alarmed. I could see from the worried expressions I caught as they flashed past, that they thought the car was out of control and a bad accident was about to happen.

Stefan was loving it. As we reached the last hundred metres of the road, he put his foot heavily on the accelerator, cranked some sort of lever near the gearbox and we surged forward, the ripples of the lake looming through the windscreen. Then, SPLASH, we were in the lake, waves washing the sides of the doors. The car had turned into a boat and we were afloat, heading towards the centre of the lake. The lever he'd pulled had produced – James Bond style – a propeller which stuck out the back and was putt-putting us past the astounded onlookers.

I have a photograph of us sitting on the top of the front seat, the wake of a speed boat showing through the windscreen ahead. It's one of my favourite photographs of Stefan. Tousled hair, carefree, full of fun. One hand on the steering wheel and the other, though a little out of the frame, gently touching mine. I found out later the car was called an amphicar and that Stefan had imported it from Germany and that it was the only one in the country.

A classic Stefan encounter.

*

But there were more to come. It wasn't long after I began our relationship that I realised I had quite likely taken on more than I could handle. Stefan very quickly drew me into his world of adventure and daring, which included extreme snow sports and, bizarrely to my mind, hunting wild animals.

My gaze fastened on the view of Mt Ruphehu, directly ahead, a 3,000-metre snow-capped active volcano, with glaciers and ski fields that still occasionally shot out fire and spewed molten lava. It was the icon of Stefan's life. So much so, that he'd had his holiday A-frame house designed so that every window captured some part of the view. There were no curtains or blinds and, in certain tricks of light around sunset, the mountain seemed to seep into the heart of the house. Sometimes I thought it was spying on me.

He'd spent countless winters since he'd arrived in New Zealand travelling overland from post-war Germany flying down its ski slopes or trudging for half a day up its vertical sides to the thermal crater lake at the summit. In those early years, he told me, it was safe to strip off and take a quick plunge into the steaming water but the temperature had changed and by the time I came on the scene it had reached boiling point and a slip on the icy banks would have ended in much the same way as a lobster ends up when thrown into a boiling pot.

The point of the trek to the crater lake for Stefan was not to linger or explore the icy peaks or marvel at the view, but to gather his strength as quickly as possible, gulp in mouthfuls of the thin air, point his skis downwards and plunge headlong into the snowy abysses for the down-hill descent. The thrill of the long, dangerous run to the foot of the mountain was his reward for the five hour trek to the top.

It was all a bit much for me, though I did go with him once. He strapped our two sets of skis over his shoulder and, with ski boots sinking into trudging the mushy snow, we trudged off, skirting around the crowds on the lower slopes and headed for the top. I lifted my gaze to the peak where the blue sky faded to a deathly white colour and thin layers of cloud swirled around like fairy floss on a stick. I was not an adept skier; in fact, I didn't care for it, the cold and constant low cloud and biting winds and sleeting snow far from my idea of a good time.

Nonetheless, I did as I always did – went along with Stefan's plans. About two-thirds of the way up the icy climb to the top, we reached a sort of no-man's-land of wide, sweeping low-slung troughs with pristine snow, not even a suggestion of a footstep or animal trail. The isolation hit me. Obviously, no one else had trodden this far.

'Come to think of it, no one knows we're here either,' I thought with alarm. It had never occurred to me to tell anyone and Stefan, of course, would have been affronted by the idea.

As I paused for breath, I could feel the radiation from the glare of the sun bouncing off the snow and hitting my face burning the skin around the edges of my snow goggles. My fingers tingled with the cold despite my leather gloves and my lips felt cracked and dry. Before long, the familiar waves of anxiety that I often felt with Stefan began to sweep through me. I took a sip from my water bottle and glanced at him a few metres ahead, body bent forward with the weight of the skis on his back.

To calm myself, I turned to stare at the view in the far distance and picked out the patchy brown and green farms and the blue expanse of the faraway town with its specks of houses and roads scattered around the edges.

The sun was beating down and my ski pants and woollen sweater were damp and clammy. I'd taken off my feather ski jacket and tied it around my waist. I glanced upwards at the peak ahead. 'At least we're over halfway,' I thought, clearly aware now of the remoteness and danger of the trek we'd undertaken.

By the time we got to the summit, it was mid-afternoon and the temperature had dropped.

Stefan stood next to me, breathless from the steepness of the last few metres. He slid the skis he'd lugged up the mountain off his back and onto the soft snow and wiped the perspiration off his face with his sleeve. 'Well, there it is. Not many people get up here to see this.' He put his arm around me. 'Make the most of it.'

We gazed down into the hollow at the crater lake with its sheer sides of snow, as treacherous as a slippery dip, disappearing into the boiling water. The colour was a magical blue-green jade that I associated with travel brochures of tropical islands but the tiny bubbles and hisses of steam ominously rising and falling in the centre, fuelled by the thermal activity below left no doubt at the ferocity of the natural elements at play. I suddenly became aware the sun was well on the way down and I realised with alarm that getting to the top was not the end of this experience. I could feel the cold seeping up my ankles and my legs beginning to feel numb. A breeze started up and I felt the wind-chill whip across my face.

I still had to get off this mountain and it was a damn long way down, it would take at least one hour if all went well. I could sense Stefan's excitement as we quickly fumbled with numb fingers to strap on our skis. He was bursting with anticipation at the thrill of the descent, the reward for his long trek.

'Just follow me, as quickly as you can. It's beginning to ice over.'

And he was gone, a slim black figure traversing, turning, traversing again, dropping lower and lower with each manoeuvre while I stood frozen with fear. I knew I had to force my skis forward. I pushed hard on my ski poles and as I slid away, I heard the sickening sound of crunchy ice as my skis skimmed over the thin layer of ice that was hitting the side of the mountain. I knew if I didn't keep ahead of it I would never make it down in one piece, there would be no traction for my skis on the slippery surface, no grip to make turns, and I would fall and God knows where I would slip and slide to a halt. The temperature was dropping by the minute and the mountain was turning into a great cone of ice. I can't say what happened next because the fear and anxiety of the moment have pretty well blocked it out. I suppose the momentum of the slippery ice kept me going and sheer will power and fear kept me from falling over.

By the time I'd reached the no-man's-land we'd encountered on the way up, I could see tiny cars in the car park below but, rather than reassuring me, they only made me aware of how much further I had to go to be safe. I was regretting the whole thing. A not uncommon thought I'd had with a number of my adventures with Stefan.

Eventually, I reached the bottom and caught up with him.

He took my hand. 'Where were you? I was looking back for you. Are you OK?'

I was shivering with fear and cold, too close to tears to answer. As he turned to strap our skis onto the car, I took off my gloves and undid my ski boots, putting them in the boot.

He stopped to gaze at the mountain in the fading light, as if lost in thought, the familiar furrows between his eyes creased in concentration. Swirls of cloud and snow drifted silently around the tops, the very peak we'd climbed, by now a cone of deadly ice. So high, so remote.

He turned to me not taking his eyes off the mountain and, in almost a whisper, said, 'It's where I want my ashes scattered.'

It was all I needed. Exhaustion hit me, the fear and frustration of the day overwhelmed me. I'd had enough. I turned towards the open car door and the comfort of the heater.

The Shame, the Shame

Stewart was a friend of mine many years ago when I lived in Wellington in New Zealand. He died some time ago. He had lived his life in a wheelchair. Polio. His legs were short and his upper body spread and sunken into the seat of his wheelchair. His permanent home. His face always had to turn up to look at you, of course, as he was sitting and everyone else was standing tall. We worked together in the Records section of a large insurance company. Wellington was not a backward city but, to put it kindly, it was also not at the forefront, even the beginning of social and workplace change. It was, in fact, well behind.

Stewart asked me to dinner one evening. There was a new teachers club and we went there. The main eating area was on level two, but it wasn't for us.

'We'll have to eat at the coffee shop on the ground floor,' he said. His hands were on the wheels of his chair, a faintly apologetic look on his face. 'They didn't put in a lift.'

I didn't know what to say, so I said nothing.

Later, he said he needed to go to the toilet. 'Back soon.' He trundled off, strong arms pushing the large wheels. He took a while.

Eventually, he wheeled back to our spot. 'They haven't made the opening of the doors wide enough. I had to get out of the chair and crawl across the floor.'

His look was calm. It seemed to me it was a statement, not a complaint. But it clanged in the air. I have never forgotten and have told the story many times.

Still do, to this day, some thirty years later.

The Meaning of Sex

Coralie took the set of *Encyclopedia Britannica* to St Vinnies today. Thirty-five books in all. It took her twelve trips from the car to the back-storage area of the Chatswood branch to deliver them. As she walked backwards and forwards through the front door with its wad of torn cloth wrapped around the handle to stop it banging, the musty old-clothes smell turned her stomach. Bins of men's ties, knitting needles with worn tips stacked in a chipped jug, stained mattresses and battered suitcases that had spent more time in garages than airports.

Bing Crosby, the star crooner of the 1940s, beamed out from a faded record album next to jigsaw puzzles, amateur paintings and broken furniture. A perky heart-shaped red satin cushion with 'I Love You' emblazoned on the front teetered on the shelf above. Then there was the good stuff. Cut glass sherry glasses, oversized pearl earrings and tarnished teaspoons in wooden boxes with sad little heads nestling on faded pink satin. Overhead, watching everything, a soft blue and cream Jesus figure. Head bent downwards.

Parting with the *EB*s has been unexpectedly harrowing for Coralie. They represented more than print and page, more than brown-bound tomes, more than the fancy custom-made bookcase with the curly posts that she got when she purchased them. When Coralie was at school in the 1950s, the *EB*s were akin to the crown jewels, the tree of knowledge, the font of privilege, wealth and affluence. A library of *EB*s in your house meant you mattered, you were important, worthy, in touch with the big end of intellectualism. No one questioned whether you ever turned the tissue thin pages, dipped into them out of curiosity or need. It was having them that mattered, as if that ensured the knowledge contained in those thirty-five books with their 36,540 pages would be automatically implanted into your brain.

The name *EB* was hardly mentioned in Coralie's house when she was growing up. They were so unobtainable, so remote, superior, so much not in her class. They spoke of Mother England, the empire and everything that working-class people like her family could never be. Their expectations of ever owning, or turning the hallowed pages, was zero. She never actually saw them in her childhood or knew anyone who had a set. She had never touched one. She knew they were out there but she never came across them.

All she knew was that the total sum of human knowledge was within those leather-bound covers with the fake gold lettering on the bindings. Those who had them had that knowledge and those who didn't were outside the tent, excluded, inferior and forever doomed to have the doors to knowledge and the meaning of all things slammed in their face forever. Privilege and opportunity, wealth and success went hand in hand with the *EBs*.

So it was that when Coralie was a young woman, in her thirties, with two young children and no husband, the *EBs* crossed her path again. High school was looming. She felt a sense of urgency. It was the 1980s. Her kids were midway through primary school, starting to get assignments, homework and needing to have questions answered. Her heart centred on the elusive *EBs*. Nothing began to matter more to her than installing a set in her house. She was determined her children would have that stream of privilege and importance that was denied her. They would turn the pages and learn the mysteries and wonders, the secrets and meanings of how the world worked, the movers and shakers, be in the inner circle, not the outer. So she rang up and a salesman came to the house. After hours. He was middle-aged, not so much trite as practised. He said all the usual things, the benefits, the history, the bountiful future the *EBs* would undoubtedly unfold, tapping into her dreams and vanities in much the same way as the Avon lady or the weight loss brochures.

'They go back to 1768,' he told her, running his hand over the fake gold crest imprinted on the cover of each volume.

A Scottish thistle? She had no idea.

The final incentive was a complimentary bookcase. Two shelves, with curly uprights to give a look of studied academia. The books fitted so tightly that not even a piece of tissue could have been squeezed between each one. Packed in shoulder to shoulder. If you applied any pressure, the whole structure shook. They started at 'A', so the first volume was Aardvark to Bay Window, progressing through to Education to Evolution, Krasnokamsk to Menadra and finishing with United to Zoroastrianism.

The salesperson appeared tired and world-weary. Coralie wondered whether he was an out-of-work schoolteacher. He seemed cynical, though smart, and had her measure from the beginning. She knew he was manipulating her when he said, 'And if they study medicine… they'll need this.' He flicked through a sheaf of coloured diagrams showing bones and muscles with bright red bits for blood contained in a bonus volume *How the Body Works*.

Coralie was sold. In any case, she had made her mind up long before he appeared, probably twenty years earlier. She had been longing all her life to reach out and touch, hold, open, turn the pages, read, learn and BECOME a person who had *EBs* in their house. Now she wanted it for her children, more than her. They cost around $2,000 (a lot in those days) which was $2,000 more than she could lay her hands on. But that wasn't going to stop her. These books were pivotal to her children's success in life and, and by hook or by crook she would have them. She quickly signed on the dotted line for the pay-if-off deal.

It took Coralie two years to become the owner of those books. She paid them off at $12 a week. Sometimes she couldn't find the money, and she got those all-too-familiar overdue notices. But she persevered and never wavered from her commitment to put those books in her house. She wrote a cheque for a few measly dollars, often less than she was supposed to, each fortnight and sent it off to the faceless *EB* people before they could come and take them away. The gas and phone bills could wait.

Her kids were pretty unimpressed. A double row of boring brown books? Oh, yeh. No pictures. No colours. No thanks. The paper was wispy and thin, like the pages of the Bible; even *EB* had to watch production costs. And they were so tightly wedged into the bookcase you had to wrestle with the whole structure to get one of the volumes out. Why bother?

During the years that followed, no one ever used them except for the occasional emergency. Times had changed and there were newer, friendlier reference books for kids. Not only that, they were easily accessible through school libraries. No one cared a damn about the *EB*s. Even her, in the end.

Over the next ten years, she relocated them to various parts of the house as they became more and more obsolete. They were heavy and it was difficult to carry the thirty-five volumes up and down stairs, into back rooms. They collected dust and every time she moved them, she thought their mock antique bookcase would shake and collapse with the indignity. They looked too prim and trim, too signed, sealed and delivered. The volumes fitted too neatly, the symmetry was so perfect, the brown-coloured binding so even, and if you did take the weight of the book in your hand, you got things like 'Lord Dunmore's war (1774): Virginia-led attack on the Shawnee Indians of Kentucky' or 'lopolith: igneous intrusion associated with a structural basin' or, perhaps, 'Global Tectonic Rock Cycle: Geologic aspect of earth's outer rock shell'. In desperation, Coralie resorted to looking up 'sex'. The thirty pages that followed went something like this,

> Since the great value of sex as distinct from reproduction is the reassortment and recombination of genes every generation, sex cells from two separate parents ordinarily give rise to the greatest variation…

It couldn't get much worse.

And then, an unthinkable happened to the *EBs*, something that the heady editors of 1768 could never have predicted. The whole thirty-five volumes which, end to end, measured over ten metres, became available on a slim twelve-centimetre CD.

Even donating them to St Vincent de Paul had been touch and go. At first they weren't interested and eventually only agreed because she had the full set. Virtually unused at that. So there they sit peeping out behind boxes of clothing, glassware, broken light fittings, hats and handbags. It didn't seem right for such dignified, aristocratic articles of bygone times to end up on the cutting room floor, so to speak. God help me, Coralie thought, I sort of grieve for them…

The Letter

The rounded, beautifully flowing handwriting peeping out from the folder I come across unexpectedly, the soft, almost translucent airmail paper. Thank heavens she wrote in biro. The words haven't faded even though the letter is many years old.

I'm shocked to realise that at first I don't recognise my mother's handwriting. It seems so beautiful, so feminine, so warm, loving (the word brings tears to my eyes). So, so…young and full of life. The beautifully scripted letter is eight pages long and had been written from Djakarta, where my parents had taken a two-year posting with the Australian government. It sounded pretty grand but my father was a tradesman and his job was not on the diplomatic staff but involved supervising building works and maintenance. He was fifty-eight years of age and my mother a few years younger. It was the first time either of them had been out of Australia.

'I see from the tone of your letter, Pookie, that you are unhappy,' the letter starts and a lump comes into my throat. Dear Pookie. My baby name. No one else calls me that. I can hear her voice. 'I'm sitting at the table…your father is having a lie-down…I tried out a new recipe,' she wrote in between paragraphs of advice on my lovelorn situation thousands and thousands of miles away.

How could she have known how wretched I felt, how lost and confused I was at the avalanche of grief and pain I was drowning in with the collapse of my marriage? How could I have explained when I couldn't understand myself?

Her life had been free of the pitfalls I had fallen into, the black hole I was now in with the bottom nowhere in sight. I'd reached out in a letter to my mother as my need and unhappiness intensified but I knew there was little hope she could help. The world I had created for myself would be totally foreign to her.

It probably wasn't very good advice she gave. It was naïve, directed at a life I had mistakenly taken which was beyond her experience but she was reaching out, sending me the one thing she always gave. Support and love. The words jump out at me with energy and life as I read each line. I am drawn into them, the words, the page, the world, the feeling she has recreated after all these years flood over me like I've been coloured in. Filled up. I hear the sound of her laugh. I see her blonde hair, her smile, her eyes, her twinkle, her joy, her fun. It's like she is standing next to me. I can even imagine the dress she would have been wearing, the generous proportions of her body.

I decide to give into the tears. And, whoosh, the melancholy bounds in through the open windows and hits me with a wallop. It's too late. I'm in for it now.

The letter is drawing to an end. I find myself wondering how it will finish, what endearment that she writes will tear my heart apart. I try to prepare myself, steel myself for yet another goodbye. As it happens, it's not too bad. Everyday. Matter of fact. 'Your father has woken up and come in and said "Hurry up." We're going out for dinner. Will have to fly.' Even ordinary, trivial things bring her back. Gently and with grace.

I lie on the bed awash with tears and look out the window. Once again, I am a twenty-five-year-old woman, full of love, freshness, life, energy, lithe and attractive, heartbroken for the love of a man I never got over. All the pain and joy twist and turn in me.

Afterwards, when I feel the old melancholy firmly nestled into place within me (it will go away, but will choose its own time), I am struck by the words she had written in the letter concerning her own mother, Louisa.

'I'm really looking forward to seeing Mum again. I hope she's still here when we get back.'

She was. But you, my own dear mother, were not to be for long. You were to die, before any of us could get to you, a year after you wrote this letter. And Louisa lived until she was ninety-four years old.

About the Author

Judith O'Connor has worked as a newspaper and magazine journalist and editor both in Australia and overseas. She has published and contributed to several books and her short stories have won various awards and been published in anthologies. She is currently writing a novel set in Eveleigh railway workshops in the 1920s. She lives in Sydney.